LAURA

MARGERY SCOTT

CLOVER RIDGE PRESS

MAIL-ORDER BRIDES OF SAPPHIRE SPRINGS

Miranda
Audra
Kathryn
Elise
Laura
Cassie

BRIDES OF COLDWATER CREEK

Josie
Sally
Anna
Beth

OTHER HISTORICAL ROMANCES

Emma's Wish
Wild Wyoming Wind
Rose: Bride of Colorado

MEDICAL ROMANCES

The Surgeon's Homecoming
Stranded with the Surgeon
The Firefighter and the Lady Doc

ROMANTIC SUSPENSE

A Time for Secrets
No One to Tell
The Stranger She Knows
A Question of Guilt

CHAPTER 1

Laura Shelton's father stood in front of the fireplace, his hands clasped behind his back.

Her mother sat in a damask-covered armchair in the corner of the room, her head bowed over the sewing needle she held in one hand and the hoop holding her embroidery in the other.

"Sit down," her father commanded as Laura entered the drawing room.

She'd been surprised when one of the maids had rapped on her bedroom door a few minutes before with a message that her father wished to see her. Immediately, the maid had stressed.

Now, taking in his rigid stance and the tension in the muscles in his jaw, Laura knew something was very wrong.

For a few moments, she didn't move as tiny tingles of apprehension rippled through her.

Her father glared at her. "Now!"

He was upset. No, she amended, taking in his rigid posture and the tension in his jaw. He was furious. But why? Try as she might, she couldn't think of anything she'd done—at least recently—that would make him so angry.

She slowly crossed to the settee near the window and perched on the edge of the cushion. "What is it, Father?"

He didn't answer immediately, his gaze resting on her mother, still sitting quietly working on her embroidery.

His gaze cut to her. "I had a visit today," he began.

Why should someone visiting him make him angry with her? "Oh?"

"Linus Wellington came to see me at the office," her father continued.

Suddenly, she knew exactly what had upset him.

"He told me he asked for your hand in marriage and you turned him down."

She had rejected Linus's proposal. She couldn't imagine being tied to a man who was so…stuffy. "Papa—"

"What were you thinking?" Her father's voice boomed, filling the room. "That's the fourth proposal you've turned down in the past six months."

"I know, but—"

"You're almost twenty years old. If you don't marry soon, you'll be too old to attract a man, and even if you do, you won't be able to give him the large family men want. Do you understand that? There are only a limited number of men in Springhill who are in a position to support you adequately."

Laura almost laughed. She was well aware of how many men there were in their small town, and how many of those men were men of means, men her father would approve of. And she couldn't bear to think of spending her life with any one of them.

"Why in heaven's name would you turn Linus down? He comes from a respectable family. He's well educated and he has an excellent future in front of him. He'd make a perfectly acceptable husband for you."

Her voice quivered as she spoke. "I don't love him."

She slid a glance at her mother, hoping she'd find understanding there and realizing within a split second that she would get no support from her.

Suddenly, her father's loud booming laughter filled the room.

Laura frowned. Why was he laughing?

He unclasped his hands and straightened. "You are a naïve young woman and you don't have the sense to know what you're doing. That is why it's up to us as your parents to take matters into our own hands."

Laura was incensed that her father had such a low opinion of her. She opened her mouth to tell him so, but his skin had taken on a reddish tinge and a vein in his temple pulsed, a sign she knew meant that he was dangerously close to losing his temper completely.

He stalked across the thick carpet to where she was sitting and towered over her. "Love has nothing to do with marriage. You need a husband who can support you. In return, you look after his home, bear his children and do what you're told. Nothing more."

Laura couldn't stay silent a moment longer. "No, Papa. I'd rather be a spinster—"

"Believe me, you do not want to spend the rest of your life as an unmarried woman, being pitied by your friends, being dependent on family or even strangers for a home. You refused Albert Dawson, William Fredericks and Charles Raton. Now you've refused Linus Wellington. How many more offers do you expect to get?"

Lowering her gaze, she spoke softly, knowing her words would be ridiculed even more. "I don't love any of them. In fact, I don't even like any of them enough to spend more than a few minutes in their company."

She raised her head and met her father's eyes. "Papa, if I must spend my life with a man, I want him to be one I can love and respect."

"You can learn to love your husband."

She shook her head. "I don't believe that," she said. "Love isn't something a person can learn to do. It's a feeling that can't be explained—"

"You're wrong," her father cut in. "Look at your mother and I. Our parents arranged our marriage and we're very happy together. Isn't that so, Maisie?"

For the first time since Laura came into the room, her mother looked up from her sewing. The sadness in her eyes belied the words that came out of her mouth. "Of course, Theodore."

Laura's father waved his arm in his wife's direction. "See? We've made a good life for ourselves—and you. Now it's time you started your own family, while you're still young enough to attract a decent man."

Laura rarely defied her parents, but this time… She stood, drawing herself to her full height, even though she barely reached her father's shoulder. "I will not marry any of those men."

Her father let out an exasperated sigh. Turning to his wife, he threw up his hands. "This is your fault," he ground out. "You let her read those…those books…"

Maisie threaded the needle into her embroidery to secure it and then set it on her lap. "What books, Theodore?"

"Those books…Jane somebody…"

"Do you mean Jane Austen?"

"Yes," he replied shortly. "I didn't approve of them, but I gave in to your pleading. If I'd forbidden you to buy them for her in the first place, we wouldn't have a daughter now with these ridiculous fanciful ideas in her head."

Laura watched the exchange between her parents with interest. She'd never known her mother to be able to convince her father of anything. She couldn't help but wonder what else went on between them that she was unaware of?

Apparently her mother had more influence with her father than she knew of. Maybe her mother understood how she felt. "Mother…"

Her mother's voice was soft and gentle when she spoke. "Theodore…" she began. "I think—"

"I will not have it!" Her father slammed his hand on the fluted walnut table beside the chair. Her mother's china teacup rattled in the saucer. "I've let you deal with her until now and look at where we are. You will stay out of this."

He spun around and glared at Laura. "If you're determined to only marry for love, then be my guest. Go and find the man you can love, but I expect you to be married before the end of the year."

"What?" Where was she going to find a husband so quickly, especially since she rarely left Springhill? Laura spun around to face her mother. Surely she would find support there, especially since it seemed her mother had never found love. "Mother…"

"I'm sorry, Laura." Her mother's soft voice was like a death knell to Laura. With a sympathetic shake of her head, her mother returned to her sewing.

"I'm not going to coddle you one minute more," her father spat out. "Both of your sisters found suitable husbands, even Edith, and she's two years younger than you. Either you find a husband and marry before the new year, or I will find one for you and you will marry him."

Anger surged through her. Could he really force her to marry someone? She wasn't sure, and even though she knew she should keep quiet, when she got angry, she tended to ignore her good sense. Raising herself to her full height, which even then barely reached her father's shoulder, she met his gaze defiantly. "And if I refuse?"

"Then you'll find somewhere else to live and another way to support yourself, because you will no longer be welcome in this house."

The schoolhouse door opened just as George Cowan dismounted and tied his horse to the hitching post. Children poured out, their excited voices and laughter filling the air as they raced down the steps and scattered.

Where was Alice? he wondered. Was she being kept behind? The thought had just crossed his mind when his six-year-old daughter appeared in the open doorway. As usual, the hem of her dress was dirty, she had a bluish stain on her apron, and her hair had come loose from the pigtails he'd spent so much time taming that morning. He watched as she jumped from the top step to the ground and hurried over to where he was waiting.

"Papa," she said breathlessly, "my teacher says to go see her before we go home. Can I go play with Tommy? He got a new ball."

"Oh…sure…" he replied. "Don't go anywhere. I won't be long."

Alice seemed far too happy to be in trouble, but what other reason could the teacher have for wanting to see him?

His stomach churned, and for some reason he couldn't understand, he felt like a boy again and he was the one who was in trouble with his teacher. I'm a grown man, he told himself as he stepped through the door. He paused, letting his eyes adjust to the dim interior after the blinding sunshine outside. The smell of chalk and books filled his nose, bringing back memories of his days in the same schoolhouse. His gaze drifted to the third desk in the second row, which likely still had the initials GC and PJ on it that he'd carved into the wood when he was eleven years old. He'd gotten taken out to the woodshed for what he'd done, but it had been worth it at the time to show Patsy Johnson how much he loved her. He'd been so sure she was the girl he'd spend his life with. She'd disagreed, he'd been broken-hearted and he'd made a vow that he'd never ever love another girl. And then, a few years later, he'd met Verna. A soft smile tugged at his lips at the memory.

A clipped female voice burst into his musings. "Mr. Cowan."

"Yes, ma'am," he replied automatically. Even though Alice's teacher wasn't any older than he was, he'd been taught to respect ladies and authority, no matter what.

Miss Coleridge, the new teacher in town, gestured to one of the desks in the front row and then took her place at her desk. "Please sit down."

George folded himself into the chair facing her.

"Mr. Cowan," she said once George was settled, "I wanted to speak to you about Alice."

"What about her? Is she having trouble with her studies—?"

"Oh, no, not at all," the teacher interrupted. "In fact, she's one of my best students."

"Then what? Is she causing trouble?"

"No." She paused, as if she were trying to figure out what to say next.

"Begging your pardon, ma'am, but you didn't ask me to come in here to talk about the weather, so whatever you've got to say, don't you think it's best to just spit it out so we can get it out in the open?"

She smiled softly. "You're absolutely right, and I apologize. First, let me say that Alice is a delightful child, bright, friendly and full of energy."

He already knew that. "So, what's the problem?"

"She's…acting more like a boy than a girl."

"Oh." George really didn't know what else he could say. He'd expected to hear that she was lagging in her studies, or that she wasn't behaving herself, but this…

"She tells me her mother has passed…"

George still had trouble thinking about Verna without a lump forming in his throat. "That's right," he replied.

"I'm sorry for your loss," the teacher said. "It's difficult for a girl to lose her mother at such a young age."

"I do the best I can, but there aren't any women at the ranch. When she's not here at school, she spends her time with me or the boys."

"I understand, and in that case, it's understandable that she's the way she is." The teacher rose and moved to sit down on the chair beside him. "Mr. Cowan, all Alice's friends at school are boys. At recess, instead of playing with dolls or jumping rope with the girls, she's either playing marbles with the boys, or climbing trees, or—"

George held up his hand. "You don't have to tell me," he admitted. "I know what she's like."

Miss Coleridge let out a soft sigh. "I know it's difficult for a man to raise a young girl, but if she continues the way she's going, she'll never grow up to be a lady. And if that happens, she won't have the skills to care for a home and family or her own, even if she can find a man who's willing to marry her."

George slumped against the back of the chair and glanced out the window to the fields beyond. He was failing as a father, but he didn't know what he could do about that. He couldn't teach her about the things girls needed to know.

Mrs. Lazlo, the housekeeper he'd hired the month before, had told him she didn't like children and had made it clear that looking after Alice wasn't part of her job. Still, he'd hired her because she was the only housekeeper he'd been able to find who was willing to come to the ranch. Her employment had lasted until the week before when she'd walked out without even giving him a chance to find a replacement.

"I hate to even suggest it, but Alice needs a mother."

George's eyes widened. No other woman could ever take Verna's place. At her funeral, the pastor had told him that time would ease his grief, and he did admit that he didn't miss her quite as much as he did at first. But he sure wasn't ready to go courting again. "Miss Coleridge, I appreciate the advice, but I'm not ready to even thinking about marrying again."

"If you aren't ready to marry for your own sake, do it for Alice's. I'm not one to gossip, and it's none of my business, but…"

"But what?" George asked.

Miss Coleridge didn't speak immediately. "I want to choose my words carefully, because I shouldn't criticize, but I do know Mrs. Lazlo. While she may keep your house well, you may find that in time, her… temperament…will affect Alice."

George had wondered the same thing, but finding another housekeeper was next to impossible. It had taken weeks to even find Mrs. Lazlo.

"Mr. Cowan," the teacher said softly, "the sooner Alice has a woman's influence, that is, a woman who loves her, the better off she'll be."

CHAPTER 2

"Miss Coleridge is a nice lady," Alice said once George settled her in the wagon and they began the drive back to the ranch, "but she says I need to bring a doll to school for recess."

George glanced over at his little girl, his heart full. She looked so much like Verna that sometimes it took his breath away. Was he really hurting her by not marrying again?

"She said I should bring a doll to school for recess tomorrow," Alice repeated.

The teacher had already tried to lead Alice into more female territory. He wasn't sure he liked the thought of someone else influencing her but at the same time, he knew she was trying to help his daughter. "Why don't you take the doll your mama bought for you?"

Alice looked up at him, her nose scrunched and

her brows meeting in the middle. "I'm not going to play with a doll. I'm going to play baseball."

He didn't respond. What was he going to say? He could force her to take the doll, but he couldn't force her to play with it.

Beside him, Alice chattered on about her day at school. "I ran so fast, Papa," she said, grinning widely as she told him about the race she'd won against a boy who was older than she was. "And he has long legs."

She swung her legs as she spoke, and George noticed a hole in the knee of one of her stockings. "What happened to your stocking?"

She looked down at her legs as if she'd never seen the hole before. Then she met his gaze. "I fell down."

George wasn't surprised. Alice seem to fall at least once a day, usually because she wasn't paying attention to what she was doing or where she was going. Now she had a hole in her stocking he'd have to try to mend. Just one more chore to add to the list of things that needed to be done since he had no wife and Mrs. Lazlo had made a point of telling him her job was to cook, to clean and to do laundry. Nothing else.

"We was playing hide and seek, and I tripped over a rock," she went on.

"You need to be more careful," he said. "One of these times you're going to really hurt yourself."

She shifted, lifting her leg onto his lap. "See? I didn't hurt myself. It didn't even bleed."

"This time," he muttered to himself.

They'd driven a few minutes more when Alice

grabbed his arm. "Look, Papa," she shouted, pointing to the shrubs and trees that lined the trail.

George's gaze followed her outstretched finger. "What? I don't see anything."

"It's a squirrel, and it has something in its mouth. It ran away but I want to go see where it went."

If he had time, he would stop and they'd go for a short walk in the woods, but right now, he needed to get back to the ranch to finish up chores and make supper. "We don't have time right now," George told her.

"But I want to see the squirrel," Alice whined. She slumped down in the seat, folded her arms across her tiny body and glared at him.

He ignored the look she gave him. "And you'll want supper, won't you?" he asked, smiling at her. "I bet you're hungry."

She nodded. "Can I have a cookie when we get home?"

"One," he said, "but only if you promise to eat all your supper."

"I will," she replied, nodding at the same time. "And then after supper, can you show me how to play poker?"

Had he heard her right? "What?"

She let out a sigh. "Don't you know how? It's a game with cards."

"I know what it is," he told her. "How do you know what it is?"

"I seen Dutch and Marty and Pinky and Jed

playing with cards yesterday when they was sitting outside after supper."

"You did?"

She nodded, her pale blonde ringlets bouncing with every movement. "There was dollars and nickels and quarters, too. Lots of them. I asked them what they was playing and Dutch said they was playing poker. So can you show me how to play? I don't got dollars but I have three pennies."

He'd tried not to think about Miss Coleridge's words, but suddenly, he realized the woman was right. Alice had been hanging around with men far too much, and if he didn't do something about it—soon—Heaven only knew what she'd want to try next. Smoking cigars? Alcohol?

"So can you, Papa?" Alice's voice interrupted his thoughts. "I want to play poker."

"Poker is not a game for little girls," he said.

"Why not? Is it a game for little boys?" she asked, cocking her head to the side the way her mother always had when she didn't quite understand the answer to a question.

"No," he replied, "it's not a game for little boys either. It's a game for grown men."

"But you said grown people don't play games."

He had said that once when Alice had been pestering him to play stickball. He'd have to remember his daughter had a memory like an elephant.

"Grown men do play cards."

"Grown ladies don't get to play cards?"

He shook his head. "No."

"Why not?"

He thought for a few seconds, and coming up with no logical reason why not, he shook his head. "They just don't," he said, "and I will not teach you to play poker."

Alice didn't ask again, and thankfully, she forgot about poker and spent the rest of the ride home chattering about one of the students who'd spent the day in the corner for putting a bug in Betty Lou's desk.

When he finally sat down after tucking Alice into bed for the night, his thoughts returned to his most pressing problem—Alice's boyish ways.

He could probably try to hire a housekeeper, but a housekeeper wasn't permanent. For weeks after Verna died, Alice was inconsolable. It had only been the past few months that she'd started to become the happy little girl she was before. He couldn't put her through that again with a housekeeper who might not stay.

No, he decided, there was nothing else to do but find himself a wife. The question was, where would he find one? There were very few available females in Sapphire Springs, and he wouldn't entrust the most important person in his life to any of them.

He knew a few men who'd gone to Miranda Weaver for help in finding a wife, and as he climbed into bed a short time later, he decided he'd head into town in the morning and see what he had to do to get himself a bride.

"A few more little tucks here and there should do it," Earleen, the owner of Madame Renault's Fashion Emporium, said, pinching the silk gown Laura was wearing. "You're going to look magnificent in this color."

Laura gazed at herself in the mirror as Earleen added another pin to tighten the waist of the gown. The ruby red silk did contrast against Laura's creamy skin and her blonde hair. She was pleased with her choice and couldn't wait to wear it to the Autumn Nights Ball the next week.

She hoped there would be a few eligible men there from some of the neighboring towns. It had been almost two weeks since her father had issued his threat and she was no closer to finding a husband than she'd been before.

"There," Earleen said, getting to her feet after adjusting the hem. Quickly, she unbuttoned the back of the gown and slipped it off Laura's shoulders, letting it fall in a puddle on the rug.

Laura stepped out of the gown and Earleen picked it up and draped it over a chair while Laura slipped back into the blue day dress she'd been wearing earlier.

"I'll leave this for Minnie to finish off," Earleen said.

"What?" Laura's eyes widened. "Minnie? Why?" Minnie wasn't half the seamstress Earleen was, and

Laura couldn't afford to look anything less than perfect at the ball. Her whole future was at stake.

Earleen had been designing and making Laura's clothes for the past five years, and over that time, Laura felt as if they'd become friends. They didn't socialize with each other, but theirs was a relationship that was definitely more than a merchant and customer.

A tinge of pink flushed Earleen's cheeks. "I've sold the shop and I'm leaving town tomorrow."

"But…where are you going? You know I don't trust anyone else."

Earleen's eyes sparkled. "I'm going to Wyoming," she said dreamily. "I'm getting married."

"Married?" Laura reached out and wrapped her arms around Earleen in a hug. "I'm so happy for you, even though I know I'll never find anyone else who sews as well as you do."

"Minnie just needs more practice," Earleen assured her.

Laura dropped to a settee. "I'm not sure I believe you, but she'll have to do. Now, tell me everything. Where did you meet someone from Wyoming?"

Earleen untied the pincushion she'd had attached to her wrist and set it on the table. "I haven't exactly met him yet."

Laura was confused. She was getting married but hadn't met the groom?

"I answered an advertisement in the newspaper for a bride," Earleen went on.

"The newspaper? I admit I rarely look at a newspaper except once in a while if there's something I want to see in the society pages," Laura commented.

Earleen moved toward the door. "I'll show you," she said, disappearing and returning a few seconds later with a newspaper in her hand. Opening it on the table, she leafed through the pages until she came to a page near the back. "Here. Look."

Laura crossed to the table and scanned the page of small advertisements—ranchers, merchants, men who didn't mention how they made their living, all looking for a bride. "Unbelievable," she murmured.

"This is an old newspaper, but there are advertisements like that in all the newspapers these days. There's even a newspaper called the Matrimonial Times full of advertisements from men all over the country seeking brides," Earleen pointed out.

"How interesting." She'd heard about mail-order brides, but she'd never known anyone to risk traveling across the country to marry a man she'd never even seen.

"Ray and I have corresponded for a few months now," Earleen went on. "He proposed marriage and sent me a train ticket to come to Wyoming. We'll be married as soon as I get there."

It all sounded so dangerous, but at the same time, exciting. Still, men being men… "But…what if he drinks too much, or gambles, or beats you? What if he's a…monster?"

Earleen shrugged. "I'm willing to take the chance.

I'm not getting any younger. He seems like a good man. If I want to have a home and children instead of living in a boarding house for the rest of my life, I have to hope he's as good in person as he sounds in his letters."

Laura hugged Earleen again. "Then I wish you well and hope you have years of happiness together."

"Thank you," Earleen said softly.

The sun had disappeared behind a cloud by the time Laura bade Earleen a final goodbye and she left the shop. She strolled down the cobblestone street toward her family's home, her mind whirling with thoughts of other towns with so many available men and hers with so few.

She was running out of time. She knew that. She'd yet to find a man who attracted her in a romantic way, and even if she did find one soon, she had to have enough time for him to fall in love and be married by year's end.

The ball the next week was likely her last chance.

CHAPTER 3

George dried his sweaty hands on his pant legs, then opened the door of the Blue Sapphire Diner and went inside before he had time to change his mind.

Mouth-watering aromas met his nose. Bread baking, apples and cinnamon blending with roasting chicken, made his mouth water. He hoped that once he found a wife, his house would smell like this, too.

He couldn't picture sharing his life with another woman, but he also knew Alice's teacher was right. Alice needed a woman's influence, if not now, then definitely later as she grew up and became a woman.

She was still young enough that she'd probably accept another woman as her mother. When one of his friends had remarried the year before and brought her home to his two older children, there'd been nothing but chaos and misery until the woman left.

There might be a period of adjustment when he brought another woman into the house, but with any luck, she would be able to quickly build a relationship with Alice, and even though there would be no 'real' marriage between him and his new bride, they would be able to live in harmony and with friendship and respect.

"Good afternoon, George." Miranda Weaver snaked her way through the tables toward him. "We haven't seen you much lately. How are things out at the ranch?"

George nodded. "Fine. Just fine."

"It's a bit early for supper, but I do have a pie that just came out of the oven—"

"Thanks, but I'm not here to eat," he said. "I…I heard you've been finding wives for some of the men in town."

Miranda smiled. "That's right. Are you interested in marrying again?"

He wasn't, but he didn't quite know how to explain to Miranda that he only wanted a woman to cook, clean, and be a mother. He didn't need anything else. "To be honest, I'm not looking for another woman to…" He didn't embarrass easily, but he felt the blood rush to his face. Talking about things like marriage to a woman was…awkward, to say the least.

"To love?" Miranda voiced the word he hadn't been able to bring himself to say.

He nodded. "Were the other men you helped looking for a real marriage?"

"Heavens, no," Miranda replied. "In fact, a few told me straight out that they only want a housekeeper and nothing else. Strangely enough, some of those men were the first to fall in love with their new brides and are living very happily together now."

"I'm still not sure this is the right thing to do," he muttered, "but it would be nice to not have to worry about cooking and cleaning, but mostly I'm doing this because Alice needs a mother. Right now, there's only me and the ranch hands at home, and she needs a woman to help her grow up right."

"I'm not busy right now, so why don't you sit down," she said, pulling out a chair at the closest table. "I'll get you a cup of coffee and we'll talk about it so that you feel more confident in whatever decision you make when we're finished."

A half hour later, George left the diner after having asked Miranda to place the ads that would hopefully bring him a new bride.

Laura paced the plush carpet in her bedroom the day after the Summer Nights Ball. "The ball was a disaster," she complained to her best friend, May Deline, who was curled up on the window seat that looked out onto the garden. "A complete disaster."

"How could it be so bad?" May asked. "Didn't you have dance partners?"

Laura plopped down into a brocade chair beside her bed. "Oh, I had a partner for every dance, but there were very few men there that I didn't already know, and the ones I didn't know, I couldn't bear to look at across a breakfast table every day for the rest of my life. I finally invented a headache so that I'd have an excuse to leave and go home."

May got up and crossed to the tray holding a silver tea service and a cake stand piled high with cookies and cakes. She plucked a petit four off the plate and took a bite, letting out a sigh of pleasure. "You don't have much time to find a beau and marry him before the holiday season," she said, she said as she set the rest of the pastry on a small plate. "What are you going to do?"

Laura had lain awake most of the night asking herself the same question. Since it would be impossible to find a suitable husband in Springhill, she had no choice but to search elsewhere.

As the first rays of dawn peeked through the curtains at her window, she happened to notice the gown she'd worn the night before and she'd left in a heap on the floor when she got home.

Suddenly, the answer had become crystal clear.

"I'm going to become a mail-order bride," she announced.

May choked on the last piece of the petit four in her mouth.

Laura rushed to her side, patting her back until she could catch her breath.

May took a lace-trimmed handkerchief out of her pocket to dab the tears in her eyes. "Did I really hear you?" she croaked once she could speak again.

Laura nodded. "And you must help me choose my husband."

"I will do no such thing," May said, shaking her head, her dark auburn curls whipping around her face. "Why would you even think of marrying a man you've never met?"

Laura had wondered that herself, but when she'd considered the consequences if she didn't marry by the end of the year, she'd decided it was worth the risk.

"There is not one man in this town who I could stand being tied to for the rest of my life," she pointed out, "and I have no doubt my father will carry out his threat if I refuse, so I really have no choice. A stranger can't be any worse than..." Her nose crinkled in disgust. "Linus. It's worth the gamble."

May plucked another petit four from the plate and popped the whole thing into her mouth, then washed it down with her tea before she spoke again. "This is such a bad idea."

"That may be," Laura replied, "but it's what I'm going to do. I'd like you to help me, but if you won't, I will choose myself."

That morning, after having breakfast with her parents, Laura had casually asked her father for the newspaper when he was finished with it. He'd folded it and slid it across the table. "I'm surprised you want to read a newspaper," he'd said with a chuckle.

"It's for May," she'd lied. "She's coming to visit this afternoon and she needs newspapers for some art thing she's doing."

"That girl has always been a little strange," Laura's mother had commented as she buttered a slice of bread. "I honestly don't see how the two of you can be such good friends. You have nothing in common."

Laura hadn't bothered to answer. At least her parents hadn't forbidden her to associate with May the way they had with a few other friends she'd had over the years.

"What happened to you last night?" May asked, drawing Laura back to the present. "You really have gone mad."

"I'm not mad at all," Laura said. "I'm not giving my father the opportunity to make my decisions for me."

Laura crossed the room and picked up the newspaper, bringing it back with her to the table. She moved the silver tray out of the way and opened the newspaper to the page she'd been studying all morning.

"What is this?" May asked, coming to stand beside her.

Laura studied the newspaper again, paying particular attention to several advertisements she'd circled earlier with a pencil. "I spent all morning reading every one of the advertisements. Some were unbelievably rude and scandalous…"

"Really?" May sounded intrigued. "Worse than *Fanny Hill?*"

Laura shrugged. "I don't know. I've heard of it, but I've never read it."

"I have." May grinned.

Laura's eyes widened and her words came out on a gasp.

"You haven't."

May nodded. "I overheard one of the maids who work at the hotel talking about it one day when I was at the market so I found a copy and read it in bed after I knew Grandmother was asleep."

"And you didn't tell me?" Laura tried to sound annoyed that her friend hadn't confided in her, but she couldn't contain her smile.

"I meant to, but I forgot," May replied. "Show me one of the advertisements and I'll tell you how shameful it really is."

Laura pointed to one small paragraph and read it again while May did the same.

When she was finished reading, May straightened. "I'd say this man should be dealt with the way my grandfather used to deal with aggressive animals before he died."

"My thoughts exactly," Laura said. "Now help me to choose a husband from the ads I've circled."

For the next hour, Laura and May pored over the

newspaper until finally, they had crossed out almost every advertisement.

She couldn't say why, but something about the way one of the remaining advertisements was written drew her in. No fancy words, no conceit or demands, nothing but simple words.

My name is George Cowan. I'm a twenty-six-year-old widowed Texas rancher looking for a healthy 20-26-year-old woman willing to build a life with me and my 6-year-old daughter who seems to think she's a boy. If you are the woman who can complete this family, please respond to Mrs. Miranda Weaver, Sapphire Springs, Texas.

"Are you sure about this?" May asked. "You'd be an instant mother."

Laura nodded. "I am. This little girl needs me. She sounds like she's growing up to act and think like men, and if nothing else, I can teach her how to be feminine."

"That's true." May took the lid off the silver teapot and looked inside. "The pot's empty," she said. "Shall I ring for more?"

Laura looked up at her friend. "Yes, please," she said, smiling. "We have a letter to write and plans to make."

Turning her attention back to the newspaper on the table, she murmured, "George Cowan. Mrs. George Cowan. Laura Cowan. The name has a nice ring to it."

"It does," May agreed.

Laura got up and crossed to her writing desk,

opened the drawer and took out a sheet of paper, her pen and ink.

As she dipped the nib of her pen into the ink, she murmured to herself, "Well, Mr. Texas rancher of Sapphire Springs, Texas, you have just found your new bride."

CHAPTER 4

Two weeks later, Laura looked on as the postmaster set three envelopes on the store counter. She'd been collecting the mail from the store herself for the past few days, unsure when she might expect a letter from Texas. If Mr. Cowan even replied, she thought. He might have had several replies and had chosen someone else.

Usually, one of the maids made the trip to get the mail, but she'd offered to go, explaining that she enjoyed the walk. Her mother had seemed surprised at Laura's sudden interest in getting exercise, but just shook her head and ignored it.

"There's not much today," the postmaster commented as Laura picked up the envelopes and tucked them into her reticule.

That was obvious, Laura thought. Smiling, she muttered an agreeable comment, thanked him and hurried outside.

The temperature had dropped overnight and a brisk wind and tugged at her hair as she hurried along the street toward home.

Winter would be here soon, she thought. If Mr. Cowan's reply held an invitation to join him to Texas, she'd have to make arrangements immediately, before snow and ice made travel difficult.

She paused outside the gate in front of her house, took the envelopes out of her reticule and looked at them. Her heart thudded against her chest when she saw the letter addressed to her.

Her name was written with a heavy hand and was little more than a scrawl across the front of the envelope. Her throat dried up. Did the thick lines of ink mean he had a heavy hand elsewhere as well? The contents of this letter could change her life, but she wouldn't know until she reached her bedroom.

A gust of wind whistled through the oak trees dotting on the front lawn, tugging at her cape as she opened the gate and hurried up the stairs. She shivered, tucked the letter from Texas back into the reticule and went inside.

After handing her cape and the two letters for her father to the maid who met her in the marble-tiled foyer, she forced herself to walk slowly up the stairs to her bedroom. As soon as she closed the bedroom door, she dug into her reticule, took out the envelope and ripped it open.

She unfolded the single sheet of paper she found inside and read the words he'd written. He wanted her to come to Texas to be his bride. Well, in truth, he didn't exactly say those words, but that's what he meant. She was sure of it.

Dropping into her favorite chair near the window, she looked out the window at the dark clouds now scudding across the sky, the letter open in her hands, and her heart racing with both excitement and terror.

Somewhere deep inside, she hadn't really believed he'd write back. Now it was very real. Could she really do this? Her parents would be furious, she'd miss May and her other friends, and she'd be traveling across the country alone to marry a man she'd never met and become a mother to a child she hadn't borne.

Yet if she stayed in Springhill… She shuddered, visions of the men her father would choose from to be her husband flashing through her mind. Either that, or she'd be living on the street, fending for herself. And every woman knew what that meant. If she couldn't find employment…and really, what were the chances of her finding a job with no skills and no

references?…she'd end up like those other poor souls on Carter Street, selling their bodies for a few pennies.

She couldn't bear either one of those options, so she had no choice but to take the chance and go to Texas. But to go alone…

An idea suddenly hit her and a few minutes later, she was walking as quickly as she could—a lady running was frowned upon—toward May's small house a few blocks away.

The storm the night before had blown down a section of fence in the south pasture, snapping the posts. George and his foreman, Dutch Vanfleet, had spent the morning tracking down cattle that had strayed and keeping them contained while they dug new fence posts and replaced broken boards.

Dutch swung the hammer and hit the nail squarely on the head. "What did you go and do a fool thing like that for?" he asked when George finished telling him about his visit to town and the letter he'd written to a woman back East.

"I need somebody to keep house and look after Alice," George grabbed another board and held one end of the board in place while Dutch hammered the other end. "The sooner the better, too," he added. "I can't keep asking neighbors to watch her when I'm out here working."

Dutch shrugged. "I suppose that's true, but a woman who can't find a husband for herself must have something wrong with her, don't you think?"

"Possible, but I sure hope not," George replied. "Maybe she's shy, or maybe she lives out in the country and hasn't met any single men."

"Or maybe she's such a shrew no man wants her, or she's been in a convent, or—"

George set the last board in place. "She sounded normal in her letter, so I'm going to hope for the best."

"Well, rather you than me," Dutch said, hammering the nail into place. He picked up the bucket of nails and set it back in the wagon beside them. "I plan to stay unattached. I haven't met a woman yet who'd make me even think about settling down."

"Yet." George emphasized the word. He understood the way Dutch thought. He'd thought the same way once. And then he'd met Verna. He remembered the day as if it were yesterday.

She'd stepped down off the stage and smiled at him as he walked by on his way to the mercantile, and he'd lost his heart.

She'd come to Sapphire Springs to visit a friend, planning to spend a week or so before she went home. He at the time that she'd felt the same way, but the week became two and then three. By the time she left town a month later, he'd proposed to her and she'd accepted.

"One of these days, a woman is going to come along who's going to change your mind, maybe even before she says a word to you," George said with a laugh. "You're going to want nothing more than to spend every minute with her for the rest of your life. And I'm going to remind you of this conversation."

Dutch laughed. "That'll happen when bulls start having calves."

"Please come to Texas with me, May." Laura knew she sounded desperate, but the truth was, she *was* desperate. She couldn't imagine going so far away by herself.

May sat at the table in the kitchen of the small house she shared with her grandmother, condensation from a glass of lemonade making a puddle on the table.

Laura pointed to the table. "You'd better clean that up before your grandmother sees it. You know she'd be upset."

"Just one more thing for her to complain about," May muttered, but she quickly grabbed a towel to clean it up before it left a ring in the wood. "I don't think the woman has even gone one whole day since I got here without complaining about me and reminding me what a burden I am." She slid back into her chair after hanging up the towel to dry.

"That's why you should come with me," Laura prodded. "You know she doesn't want you here, so why stay?" She could sense May wavering, and with a little more persuasion, she was sure she could convince her friend to go with her.

May shrugged. "I don't know why I stay, but I'm certainly not going to marry a stranger, not that I've had an offer anyway. It's such a long way."

"It'll be an adventure. We'll see the country and be able to be free." Laura chuckled. "Well, you'll be free. I'll be married, but if he turns out to be a horrible man, I'll need you more than ever."

"I don't know…"

"Your grandmother will likely be happy to see you go," Laura pointed out. "You know that."

May let out a bitter laugh. "You're probably right. Almost every day she reminds me I have no prospects and I'm going to end up being a spinster she'll have to support until her dying day."

Laura smiled at her friend. She sensed May was close to giving in. "You don't have to marry anyone," Laura assured her. "Unless you want to, that is. If females are so scarce in Texas that men have to advertise for them, then surely you'll find a husband there who you'll fall madly in love with and live happily ever after."

"You are such a romantic."

"I'm being realistic," Laura contradicted. "And if you don't find a man, I'm sure you can find employment there. I have money, too, so you could even start a business, maybe a bakery or a café or—"

May held up her hands in mock surrender, but just to be sure, Laura went on. "I'm begging you, May. Please come with me so I don't have to face this alone."

May sighed, but her lips tweaked in a small smile. "All right, I'll come with you, but only because somebody will have to teach you how to cook and clean."

CHAPTER 5

George swallowed thickly as the train's whistle shattered the air moments before it appeared at the far end of the station in Austin. The wheels screeched as it came to a stop and the depot master quickly began setting steps at the doors so that passengers could exit.

His heartbeat raced and his hands were clammy, so he shoved them in his pockets.

The woman he was planning to marry was on that train, along with a friend. He hadn't even sent a letter offering marriage before he'd received one from her explaining that it was urgent that she leave immediately, and that she'd pay her own way to Texas. That way, if he no longer wanted to marry her, she wouldn't owe him anything.

He had to admit she had at least two qualities he admired in a woman—one who went after what she wanted, and one who didn't like to be beholden to anyone.

But would she be too independent, too unwilling to give him the respect he was due as the man of the house?

He looked on, watching as the passengers disembarked and were greeted by those meeting them before they got their baggage and left the station.

Only a few passengers were left when he looked past a family greeting a well-dressed young man and saw two young women standing on the platform. They had to be Laura Shelton and her friend. Both were beautiful, elegantly dressed and even though they'd been traveling for days, looked as if they'd just stepped out of their homes and were on their way to a tea party.

One, the smaller of the two, met his gaze and smiled. Under a midnight blue hat with white ribbons and lace and tied with a bow beneath her chin, her hair, the color of cornsilk after a rainstorm, was parted in the middle and drawn away from her face. He couldn't see the color of her eyes at that distance, but he did see an expression he took to be kindness and curiosity in them. A dark blue traveling suit she was wearing hugged her generous curves.

Something stirred inside him. Was it only because he'd been without a woman for so long? His gaze switched to her companion—taller, not quite as slender, with light brown hair and the same elegant-looking clothes. While she was pretty as well, his insides didn't react to her.

The question was, which one was Laura Shelton? He'd felt an instant attraction to the blonde-haired woman, but marriage to a woman who he felt no attraction to would be easier to live with. His stomach tightened as he made his way along the platform to where the two women were standing.

The fair-haired woman met his gaze as he approached, her gold-brown eyes searching his face. "Mr. Cowan?"

"I am."

"I'm Laura Shelton," she said, holding out her gloved hand. He swore to himself. Fate had just played another cruel joke on him, sending a woman he already found appealing.

George took her hand and gently shook it, noticing how his work-roughened fingers wrapped around hers. Her heat warmed him even though the lace glove.

Laura's eyes met his, as if she'd felt it, too, but she pulled her hand away and tucked it into the other woman's elbow. "And I'd like to introduce my friend, May Deline."

He knew he shouldn't judge anyone by appearance alone, but seeing how this woman held herself and the way she spoke, he had a feeling she was the perfect woman to be Alice's mother. This woman could teach his daughter how to be a lady. "I'm happy to meet you both," he said.

May shook his hand as well and then took a step away, as if she were trying to give him and Laura room to speak privately. At this point, there was nothing to say that couldn't be said in public. "I hope the trip wasn't too uncomfortable for you both," he said, making sure May could hear that he was including her in the conversation.

"It wasn't overly pleasant," Laura said with a chuckle, "but it would have been so much worse if May hadn't been with me. We both thoroughly enjoyed seeing the countryside and the different land-scapes of this vast country as they changed from day to day."

George smiled at May. "Then I need to give my thanks to Miss Deline for accompanying you. Now you must be ready for the journey to end. It's a two-hour trip to Sapphire Springs, so if you'll tell me where to get your baggage, I'll load it into the wagon and we'll get going."

Sitting beside George in the wagon as they left Austin behind, Laura's throat was parched and her heart raced. Three people on the bench seat was crowded, and even though May had offered to ride in the wagon bed, neither George nor Laura would allow it. It meant that if Laura wasn't careful, her shoulders grazed against George's when either of them moved, and when he shifted, his thigh brushed against hers.

Even though her petticoats and crinolines prevented much of the contact, it was the first time she'd ever been so close to a man and it was unsettling.

And what a man he was! During the journey to Texas, she'd convinced herself that George Cowan would be an average-looking man, probably quite a few years older than she was, possibly even balding and with the extra weight around his middle that most men seemed to have once they reached a certain age. She'd also made it clear to May that if he turned out to be as repulsive as the men who'd offered to marry her back in Michigan then she wouldn't marry him and they'd either go home or stay and find another way to support themselves.

She'd never been more wrong! Handsome wasn't the right word to describe his features. He didn't have the delicate features of most of the men she'd known, but instead, a wide forehead, strong jaw, and blue-gray eyes with long, lush eyelashes most women would envy. His skin had been bronzed by the sun, and his hair, so dark it was almost black, brushed against his shirt collar.

Beside him on the seat, she breathed in a combination of soap, leather and something she couldn't define but that she sensed was uniquely his. A very pleasant scent which was both intoxicating and relaxing at the same time.

"You both comfortable enough?" he asked, his voice so deep and rich that her nerve endings tingled.

She nodded. Forcing her thoughts away from the

butterflies flitting around in her stomach, she concentrated on the reason she was here at all. "I'm surprised you didn't bring your daughter with you to meet us," she said.

"This wagon seat isn't big enough for four of us," he pointed out with a smile. "I wouldn't want either one of you to sit in the wagon bed, and I sure couldn't let Alice sit in there. She has trouble sitting still for more than five minutes at a time. She'd be out of the wagon the minute I looked away and be off somewhere chasing squirrels or getting herself into some other kind of trouble." He laughed, the deep timbre of his voice making her smile. The sound was pleasing, and she made a mental note to make him laugh as often as possible. "She's a handful, and I sure hope she won't be too much for you."

"I'm sure it'll be fine," Laura said, although she was starting to wonder if she'd bitten off more than she could chew. "Isn't there a saying about idle hands? She sounds as if she has a curious mind, which is a good thing."

She'd hoped to meet the little girl, but she understood why he hadn't brought her. She thought back to her own childhood. She'd been much like Alice until her mother had hired a governess who'd been so strict that Laura was afraid to move without permission when the woman was in sight.

"Where is she now?"

George shook his head. "She's with Dutch, my foreman. She's used to spending time with him and the other boys and they're good with her, even though they're teaching her things I'd rather she didn't know about."

"Oh?"

"Like playing poker," George added with a wry smile. "That was the thing that finally decided me on asking Miranda to put the ad in the newspaper."

"Oh my word," Laura gasped, but she couldn't contain the smile tugging at her lips.

"Miranda was a mail-order bride as well," George went on, "and she came to Sapphire Springs to be a mama to his two little girls, so you can go to her for advice if you need to."

Laura nodded. She was glad there would be someone she could talk to about starting life with a stranger. Of course, she had May with her, but would she really understand the problems—and there were sure to be problems—that came along with marriage to a man she didn't know?

"Alice needs someone in her life, a woman, who's not going to up and leave, who'll be there for her until she's grown. She already lost her mother and I didn't want her to go through that again because a house-keeper decided to move on."

"That makes sense," she agreed. That he would make such a huge change in his life for his daughter's well-being said a lot for a man.

"As it turns out, I was right. When I told my housekeeper you were coming, she walked out. So it's a good thing I decided to get married again now rather than in another year or two when Alice was attached to her and lost her, too."

"That's true."

"What are those flowers?" May asked, pointing to the purple blooms that seemed to cover the edges of the trail. "They're so pretty."

Laura had been so entranced with George she'd forgotten May was there. George followed her gaze and shook his head. "I don't know," he replied. "I haven't paid much mind to flowers. My wife would have…"

Suddenly, his gaze flitted to Laura, an apologetic expression filling his face. "Sorry, I shouldn't be talking about her…"

Heavens, Laura, thought, they couldn't spend their lives together with him afraid to mention his deceased wife. She reached out and rested her hand on his arm for a moment, then realizing how forward it might look, drew it away. "Please don't apologize. Your wife was a large part of your life, and she was Alice's mother. I'm not going to be upset if you mention her name. Now, please tell us about the town and your life here. Neither of us has ever been out of Michigan, so we know nothing about ranches or Texas."

For the rest of the trip, George regaled them with stories about the people of Sapphire Springs and the ranch. Both Laura and May were eager listeners, until finally, he pointed to a curve in the trail ahead. "As soon as we round the bend, you'll be able to see the town. The ranch is on this side of town, so you won't be able to see it close up today. I hope you don't mind."

Laura smiled. "Not at all. Actually I'm anxious to see the ranch and to meet Alice. How far is the ranch from town?" In fact, she could barely contain her excitement at finally reaching her destination. She couldn't wait to sleep in a room that was quiet and a bed that someone else hadn't slept in the night before.

But she'd be sleeping in that bed with…George! She studied his forearms and his hands since his shirt sleeves were rolled up. Strong hands and corded, strong forearms from hard physical labor, and darkened from the sun. And once they were married, those hands…

A strange fluttering began in her stomach and seemed to travel through her veins. Warmth spread through her, and for a moment or two, she wondered if she was about to be ill. But then, she didn't feel ill. "Oh …"

George shifted in his seat, his bare arm brushing against her. "What's wrong?"

Her face flamed, even though there was no way he could tell the direction her thoughts had gone. "Nothing. Nothing at all."

He gave her a curious glance, unsettling her, making her feel as if she had to say more. "It's just…warm."

"I'm not warm at all," May commented. "Are you sure you're not ill?"

"I'm not ill." Laura's voice was sharper than she intended.

May's eyes widened at her tone, but she only smiled and patted her hand. "I'm glad."

Just as George had said, Sapphire Springs came into view a short time later, and soon after, he guided the horses to another rutted trail leading away from town.

CHAPTER 6

"They're live oaks," George told Laura when she questioned him about the trees that lined the trail and created a canopy overhead.

Laura had never seen trees with branches that spread so far from the trunks and she was mesmerized by the designs the dappled sunshine made on the ground. "Beautiful," she whispered. "Just beautiful. Don't you think so, May?"

May nodded in agreement. "I expected Texas to be different from Michigan, but I had no idea how different."

"It sure is," George said. "I was nine years old when my folks settled here, but I remember thinking I'd never seen so much open space and blue sky."

Laura had assumed George had grown up in Texas. "Where did you come from?"

"Pennsylvania," he replied. "My uncle came down

here before I was born . He built this ranch. We came later."

"What made your family decide to move here?" May asked.

George didn't answer for a few seconds, and Laura noticed the muscles in his jaw tighten. "My pa was a coal miner, him, my other two uncles and my grandfather. One day, there was an explosion in the mine. Grandpa and one of my uncles were killed."

May's hand flew to her mouth. "Oh…I'm sorry to remind you of such terrible memories."

"Please don't go on if it's too painful," Laura said softly.

George gave them both a small smile. "It's okay," he said. "It was a long time ago but I remember that day so clearly. It was the third mine accident in less than a year. My mother was terrified, sure that it was only a matter of time before my father died, too. So they packed up and slowly made their way here, Pa taking odd jobs until they had enough money to move on."

While Laura had sympathy for the tragedy that caused George's family to leave Pennsylvania, she knew he could understand how she felt about leaving everything she'd ever known behind. "That's quite an adventure, especially for a boy."

George nodded, a smile curving his lips. "It was. My uncle welcomed us into his home, and we worked the ranch alongside him, adding land and cattle until it was what it is today. He never married, so when he passed, it came to my folks, and then to me. When I die, it'll go to my children…uh…that is…if…"

A blush crept into Laura's cheeks. She couldn't speak about such things, especially with May sitting right beside her. "Mr. Cowan, I don't think—"

George seemed embarrassed and sorry that he'd even mentioned it. "Of course. My apologies. And please, call me George."

Laura couldn't think of anything else to say, so she sat quietly while May chattered about the profusion of flowers in the fields, the warm sunshine and the birds chirping in the trees.

"Oh, look, Laura," she said, grabbing Laura's arm and pointing to movement in the distant fields. "Cows."

George grinned. "We call them cattle here, even though some are cows, some are heifers and some are still calves."

Silence descended over them until they rounded the bend George had mentioned earlier and the house came into view. "There it is," George said, pride showing on his face and in his voice.

Laura studied the dwelling that was now her home. It was a two-story house built of rough-hewn logs, with three steps leading from a stone pathway to a porch that ran the length of the house and the front door.

Three dormer windows jutted out of the second floor, and she couldn't help wondering if they had window seats like her old bedroom where she could curl up with a book and read.

Several outbuildings stood nearby, and she assumed they were barns and storage sheds.

It was a long way from the house she'd grown up in, but still, this would be *her* home, where she would be in charge, where she could sit on the floor if she wanted to, or leave her sewing on the table without it being moved.

May clapped her hands in delight. "It's bigger than I thought it would be, and much bigger than my grandmother's house."

"It's so different from what I expected," Laura murmured.

George's eyes darkened and his smile faded. "I know it's not very big right now, but we can add—"

Laura twisted to meet George's eyes. She'd given him the wrong impression. "No, that's not what I meant at all. I thought it would be smaller, more like a cabin. I've seen photos of the west, and I thought… never mind. It's different, in a good way." She smiled at him, hoping he'd see that she was surprised, not disappointed.

And what surprised her most was that she wasn't disappointed. She'd grown up in what most people considered a mansion, with maids to do her bidding and all the comforts money could buy. Yet, gazing at this simple house in the middle of fields as far as the eye could see, she was excited about the future.

"If you're not too tired, I'll show you around the ranch after lunch," George said once he'd helped Laura and May out of the wagon and they were standing in front of the house.

He hadn't even thought about feeding Laura and May until a few days before when Mrs. Lazlo had walked out, letting him know in no uncertain terms that she was capable of running the house and wouldn't be taking orders from anybody.

Thankfully, when he'd run into Miranda Weaver in the mercantile while he was looking for something easy he could offer Laura and May when they got back to the ranch, she'd offered to make something and bring it out that morning.

"I'd love to see it," Laura said, her gaze scanning the pastures. Near one of the barns, a man was walking toward a fenced-in corral holding two horses, a large chestnut with white socks and a smaller, lighter-colored horse with spindly legs.

May climbed the stairs to the porch. "If you lead me to the kitchen, I'll fix us something to eat and you can show Laura around now. I can see the rest of the ranch another time."

"No need to do that," George told her, following her up the stairs. "Miranda, the woman who placed the ad in the newspaper for me, provided lunch for us. She and her husband own the diner in town."

"How nice of her," Laura exclaimed. "I'll be sure to thank her when I meet her."

"It's nothing fancy, but better than what you had on the train or in the waystations, I'll bet." Laura laughed. "I don't think it could be any worse."

The soft sound of her laughter warmed him. One of the things he'd truly missed since Verna died was a woman's laughter. While Verna's laugh was louder than Laura's, it was a pleasing sound. He hoped there would be much more laughter in his house from now on.

"Then in that case," May said, "I'm dying to get closer to the horses. Do you mind if I wander over to the corral until lunch is ready?"

George liked that idea. He hadn't been alone with Laura since they arrived, and there were things he really needed to talk to her about. Dutch was keeping Alice occupied until later that afternoon. "I don't mind at all. That's Dutch, my foreman, in the corral."

May turned to leave and had taken a few steps when Laura grabbed her arm and spun her around to face her. "You can't—"

May cut off her objection. "You and George need some time to yourselves, to talk about things," she said softly, as if she were trying to whisper.

George's lips tweaked in a small smile. The ladies hadn't yet noticed that in the silence and the wide open spaces where there were no voices or rumble of wagons, voices carried.

Then May grinned, turned away and walked briskly toward the corral, leaving Laura alone with the stranger who would soon be her husband.

"Come on," George said, cupping her elbow and ushering her up the stairs to the porch. "Let me show you the house and get lunch started."

Two rocking chairs and a small table sat on the porch, facing the vast emptiness all the way to the horizon. They were obviously for George and his daughter. "What about Alice?" Laura asked as she followed George across the porch to the front door. "Don't you have to go and get her? Won't she be hungry?"

George laughed. "No, believe me, she won't be hungry. She likes to eat in the bunkhouse with Dutch and the boys, and even though I'm hoping having you here will help her to realize she's not one of them, one more day of spending time with them won't hurt."

"Oh."

George opened the door and went inside, then turned to face Laura and took her hand, drawing her inside. "Welcome."

Laura was excited to see the inside of her new home, but as he closed the door behind them and they were truly alone, a sudden bout of shyness swept through her.

Here she was, standing in a house—her new home—alone with a man she'd met only a few hours before. He hadn't mentioned anything about a wedding or marriage. Had he decided he didn't want to marry her after all?

She'd been told all her life that she asked too many questions, that she'd be told what she needed to know, but in this case, shouldn't she be asking? If he didn't want to marry her, she wanted to know now before her reputation was ruined by staying in his home without a wedding ring on her finger.

She wrapped her ribbons on her reticule around her hand. At least she had her own money, money she could use to get her and May back to Springhill if she had to.

"This is it," George's deep voice interrupted her thoughts.

She tried to smile, but there really wasn't much to smile about. The main floor consisted of one large room. Dust motes hung in the air where sunshine beamed through a large window looking out on the fields. A small settee, two chairs and a table between them sat on a colorful hand-hooked rug facing a stone fireplace flanked by shelves on one wall.

A painting of a man and a woman hung above the fireplace. They looked…content.

"That's my uncle and his wife," George said.

"She'd already passed before we arrived but he told us so much about her I feel as if I knew her."

"She's very beautiful," Laura commented, smiling at George as he nodded in agreement.

An area at the far end of the room was set out as a dining room, complete with a table, chairs, a buffet and hutch.

"Come on into the kitchen so I can light the stove and get lunch heated."

Laura followed him into the kitchen. She was surprised that even though the room was much smaller than the kitchen at home, it seemed to have everything she'd need. A wry smile crept across her lips, because if she were being honest, she really had no idea what she'd need to put a meal together. She'd have to learn to cook, and again, she thanked God that May had agreed to come with her.

A work bench stood beside an iron cookstove on one wall. Another fireplace filled another, and shelves and a cabinet took up yet another. In the center of the room was a table and eight chairs. The wood was worn and scratched, and as she ran her finger over one deep scratch, George came to stand beside her. "This table belonged to my grandparents and my uncle had it shipped here when they passed on. Once we're married, feel free to do whatever you want with the house, but I'd appreciate it if you leave this be."

Laura gazed up at him, into his gray-blue eyes and smiled gently. "Of course I will."

"Thanks," he said, then took a box of matches off a shelf and lit the stove. "It won't take long to heat."

"What is it?" Laura asked, crossing the room to stand beside him when he took a pale blue pottery bowl out of the icebox. That same soap and leather scent filled her nose.

She peered into the bowl, recognizing tomatoes and meat, but nothing else.

"It's chili con carne."

Laura frowned. "I've never heard of it."

"It's a dish made with beef, tomatoes, beans, vegetables and spices. Some folks make it really spicy but since you probably aren't used to that, Miranda made it mild."

"I'm not," she said. "We don't use many spices in Michigan."

She repeated the name of the dish. "It sounds like a different language," she commented.

"It's Spanish. According to a legend, the first recipe was written by a nun in Spain in the 17th century and used venison or antelope."

Laura's nose wrinkled.

"Don't worry," he said, laughing. "Miranda's chili uses beef."

"I'm glad to hear that," Laura said, her frown easing. She didn't know if antelopes even existed in America, but she was almost positive she couldn't bring herself to eat it. She had tried venison once and found it distasteful.

"How did it get here?" she asked.

"According to the tales, it was brought to Texas in the 18th century by sixteen families from the Canary Islands who settled in San Antonio. The way it's made now is probably different from the way it was made then, but it doesn't matter to me. It's one of my favorites."

How could she learn to cook the dishes he liked when May was likely as ignorant as she was? It occurred to Laura that the food they ate here in Texas was likely one of many things she'd have to get used to. What else would she have to learn?

CHAPTER 7

$\mathscr{A}$wkward silence filled the room while George set the bowl in the oven. Then he busied himself taking out plates and silverware to set the table for lunch, all the while searching for the right words to bring up the reason this beautiful woman was standing in his kitchen.

"Would you like a cup of coffee?" he asked.

"I'd love one," she said. She was gazing at him with her huge blue eyes and nibbling on her bottom lip as if she was nervous, too. Finally, he swallowed against the dryness in his throat and poured coffee for them both. "While we're waiting for the food to heat, I think we should talk."

"Yes," Laura agreed. "I think so, too."

"Why don't we sit?"

Laura nodded and slid into a chair at the head of the table while George settled into the chair to her right. She clasped her hands in her lap and looked at him, a small smile on her lips.

He'd done this. He'd sent for her, and now, here she was. "I was surprised to get your telegram saying you were on your way," he said.

That he'd been surprised was an understatement. In his letter, he'd told her he wanted her to come to Texas, but he hadn't figured on her taking it upon herself to just show up, and with a friend.

"I apologize for that. Winter was coming, and I was afraid if I took the time to reply to your letter and wait for you to write back, the weather would prevent me from traveling until spring."

He supposed that much was true, and he did need a wife and a mother for Alice sooner rather than later. Still…

"I didn't expect you to buy your own train ticket, so I'll give you the money—"

"That's not necessary. In fact, if I'd waited for you to send money, I would have given it back to you when I arrived anyway. I prefer to pay my own way." She chuckled. "It's my little bit of independence."

George admired independence in a woman. It was one of the qualities that had attracted him to Verna, and now Laura.

"I don't want to owe you anything," she went on. "I also have enough money to get May and I back home if need be. I wasn't sure how you would react to us arriving unexpectedly, and I wanted to be sure we didn't find ourselves stranded."

He smiled. She wasn't just independent, she didn't act without considering the consequences. He liked that.

"Why did you decide to become a mail-order bride? From what I hear, most ladies who do that are desperate, and you obviously weren't."

She let out a small laugh, but it held no humor. "Oh, but I was."

He listened while she described the events leading up to her decision. She was from a wealthy family, yet she'd chosen to take a chance rather than live the life her parents wanted her to. He'd never known anyone to walk away from money before, and his respect for her grew a little more.

"They must have been upset when you told them you were leaving so suddenly."

"My father was so angry I was afraid he might collapse. He threatened to lock me in my room until I came to my senses, and truthfully, I worried he might have me committed to an asylum because he was sure I'd gone mad. My mother sobbed constantly from the minute I told them until I left. So you see, I had to leave while I could. I hope they'll forgive me one day."

"Give them time," he said. "The love between a parent and a child is a bond stronger than any other."

Again, silence fell between them. Laura glanced out the window toward the corral where May was leaning on one of the fence rails watching a man on horseback slowly riding the horse in circles.

George stared at the coffee in his cup for several long moments. "So…" he said finally, breaking the silence.

"So…"

"I don't know quite how to say this…"

She smiled, her golden-brown eyes meeting his. "I've found it's always best to be direct and honest, especially when it's a difficult subject you're trying to talk about."

"I suppose you're right," he agreed, nodding. "Then I'll be direct. I wasn't proposing in the letter I sent."

Laura gazed at him for a few moments, then slumped against the back of the chair. "You weren't? But you said—"

"I said that I thought you'd be a wonderful wife and mother, and that I was looking forward to getting to know you better. You took it to mean I wanted you to come to Texas and marry me. Maybe I worded it wrong—"

She bounded up and turned away from him, but not before he noticed how her cheeks had flushed and her eyes sparkled with unshed tears. "I see," she said quietly as she stood at the kitchen window and looked outside.

He'd hurt her. He knew that, but it was better to have everything out in the open, wasn't it? "I wasn't trying to mislead you," he said. "I'm not good with words and I'm not much for letter writing. It's hard to write down what I want to say sometimes. I planned to get to know you better through letters first so we'd both know what we were getting into. What we both wanted."

She spun around to face him. "And what exactly do you want?"

"You asked for honest, then I'll be honest," he said. "I want a woman who will take care of the house, cook decent meals and who'll be a good mother to Alice. If we could be friends as well, that would do. I don't need you to love me, and I hope you don't expect me to love you, because I won't."

"I see." Her teeth worried her bottom lip as she began to pace the length of the kitchen.

George watched her move about the room. He'd thought about telling her he'd like her to share his bed, but since he wasn't willing or able to offer her love, he'd decided to keep quiet. "So you really just wanted a housekeeper," she said finally, stopping in front of him and looking down at him.

"I wouldn't put it that way…" he began.

"Oh?" Her head tilted to the side, a quirk of hers he'd found adorable when she'd done it a few times on the way to town when she had a question. "What other way would you put it? You want someone to cook, clean, do your laundry and take care of your daughter."

Guilt like he'd never known before gnawed at him. "I'm sorry, but you're right," he said. "I got so caught up in finding a good mother for Alice that I was only thinking about what I wanted. I didn't really think about what my bride might want or expect from me."

A smile creased her lips but it didn't reach her eyes. "Well," she said, "the joke is on you, because I can't do any of those things."

"You can't?"

She shook her head. "I can help you raise Alice to be a proper young lady, but that's all. I don't know how to cook unless you're willing to live on porridge and toast. I've never cleaned anything, and as for laundry, I've never even seen clothes being laundered. Dirty clothes disappeared from my bedroom and reappeared clean, pressed and folded or hung up in the wardrobe."

What was he supposed to do now? He could send her away, but even as the thought crossed his mind, he knew he wouldn't. He was drawn to her in a way he'd never thought he'd ever feel again, and even though he already wanted to kiss her, touch her, make love to her, it was more than just a physical reaction. She was a woman who'd given up her family to travel across the country in search of love. It bothered him that love was one thing he wasn't able to give her.

"I suppose this is why letters before a mail-order marriage are important," he said.

She nodded. "That's why you should marry May instead."

"What?"

Her chin quivered and he saw those tears fill her

eyes again, but only for a moment before she walked out of the room.

Laura blinked back the tears threatening to overflow as she opened the door and stepped out onto the porch. What was she thinking, offering up May instead of herself as George's wife?

She'd been honest in telling him her about her abilities, or rather her lack of abilities, but if he married May, Laura would be left to fend for herself. And Heaven knew she had no skills to find employment elsewhere. She'd have to go back to Springhill…

The tears flowed then. She couldn't go back. She couldn't marry Linus or any of the other men she knew her father had in mind.

The door opened and George's footsteps sounded on the wooden porch floor as he came to stand beside her. Without a word, he reached into his pocket and drew out a handkerchief.

When he offered it to her, she took it and dabbed at her eyes. Laura knew she wasn't an attractive crier, not like May, who was even prettier when her eyes were misty with tears and her cheeks were flushed, so she kept her face averted, focusing on the high grass waving in the soft breeze and the sound of birds chirping in the trees.

"I'm sorry," he said, his deep voice soft. "I didn't even ask what you wanted."

What did she want? She'd known he'd expect her to keep house and take care of his daughter, but what did she want from him? She really didn't know. She wanted to be treated well, of course. She wanted security. She wanted… Heat rose in her cheeks. She even wanted to discover what she'd heard about marriage. Everything. And yes, she wanted love, but she wouldn't tell him that.

Deep down she'd hoped that one day, she and her husband would fall in love and be happy growing old together, raising a family. It seemed that was something he wasn't willing to do.

She lifted her eyes to meet his bluish-gray ones, more gray than blue right now. "I want security, respect and friendship. Nothing more," she lied.

George sniffed. "I think we need to work this out, but right now, I think I smell something burning."

Thankfully, nothing was burning when George ushered Laura back inside to check on the food in the oven. What he'd smelled was a little chili that had bubbled over.

His insides tensed as he watched Laura move to the window, her hair glistening in the sunshine streaming through the window. She was small, but every curve was in perfect proportion to her height.

"I can get you a room for you at the hotel for a

few days in case you want to wait until we get to know each other a little better."

"That's very kind of you," Laura said.

"Now that May is with you as a chaperone, though, the busybodies in town won't have anything to say, so you can stay here if you want to until the wedding or I'll take you both to town after lunch. Or if you've changed your mind—"

Laura closed the gap between them. "I haven't." A frown suddenly marred her forehead. "Have you?"

Hell no! "No."

"Do you want to wait until we get to know each other so that you're sure?" she asked.

He shook his head. He'd wanted a woman who was proper and ladylike who could be a good mother to Alice. He hadn't wanted a woman who would remind him that he was a red-blooded man who hadn't had a woman since his wife died. What he'd gotten was a woman who was beautiful to look at, who had curves in all the right places, and who brought his senses back to life in a way he'd never expected to feel again.

He hadn't mentioned having a real marriage, but he did want that. Did she? Did she want children of her own? They hadn't talked about that. But then, he hadn't expected her to be here so soon. Once he'd made the decision to marry again, he'd been anxious to get it done and over with, but he'd planned to write at least a letter or two so that they could get to know each other a little before he suggested marriage.

Instead, she'd taken his letter as an invitation to come to Texas and be his wife. He still couldn't figure out where she'd gotten that impression from the words he'd written, but it didn't matter now.

"I spoke to Reverend Ford when I got your letter," he said. "He agreed to marry us whenever we're ready. Are you willing to get married in the pastor's house, or do you really want a church wedding?"

"It doesn't matter," she replied. Her voice softened and she clasped her hands in front of her. "I'd always thought I'd be married in the church I was baptized in, surrounded by friends and family, so now…"

"Are you sure you want to do this?" he prodded. He hoped she did, but he'd understand if she'd changed her mind.

She nodded and gave him a weak smile. "I do have May here, so whatever's best for you is fine with me."

"In that case," he said. "I'd like to get married tomorrow."

Laura nodded. "Then tomorrow it is."

George popped the last bite of cornbread into his mouth, washed it down with coffee, and leaned back in his chair.

May had come back to the house just as he was taking the chili out of the oven. She sniffed appreciatively when she came inside and repeated what he'd told Laura about the history of the dish they were going to eat.

Miranda had also made a pan of cornbread which he cut into squares and set on a plate.

"This is delicious," May exclaimed after she swallowed her first spoonful of the chili a short time later.

Laura nodded in agreement, her mouth full. The slightly spicy dish made her mouth tingle and her taste buds come alive. She'd already tried the cornbread, and while she found it a little dry, once she slathered it with butter, she enjoyed it.

"Do you think Mrs. Weaver would be willing to share the recipe?" May asked between spoonfuls.

"I'm sure she would," George replied. "Miranda is an excellent cook and even though she cooks everything in big batches for the diner, I'm sure that between the two of you, you can figure out what you'd need for only a few people. Do you like to cook?"

May grinned. "I do."

George slid a glance at Laura and raised his brows, silently asking the same question.

"I haven't had much practice cooking, but I'm willing to learn, and May has offered to teach me what I need to know," Laura said, spooning the last of the chili in her bowl into her mouth.

For the rest of the meal, they talked about the town, the ranch, Laura and May's trip west.

"If all the food in Texas tastes as good as this, I'll have to find a dressmaker to let out the seams on all my dresses," Laura said, chuckling as she set her spoon in the empty bowl.

"You're right," May agreed. "I can feel the pounds creeping on already."

George gazed at Laura across the table, daintily dabbing her mouth with a napkin before she folded it carefully and set it on the table beside the empty cornbread plate. She was even more than he could have hoped for. She was a lady through and through, from her dainty movements to her soft speech.

It had never occurred to him that the woman he'd

proposed to would be beautiful. Too beautiful, with that hair that he wanted to sink his fingers into and those lips he already wanted to kiss.

Most of the time, he'd accepted Verna's death, but until that morning, he hadn't believed it was even possible to be attracted to another woman. Laura had proved him wrong.

George got up and took the dishes and silverware to the sink where he set them in a basin, then poured boiling water over them. "We can deal with these later," he said, moving to the stove. "Would either of you like coffee?"

Both women declined.

"Then are you ready to see the rest of the ranch and meet Alice?"

A few wispy clouds marred the deep blue sky when Laura, May and George left the house after he showed them the rest of the house. In the distance, cattle wandered freely in the distant fields and a faint scent of pine carried in the soft breeze.

As they strolled toward the barn and the other outbuildings, George told them more about the ranch. "It's small, only a thousand acres, but it's big enough."

Laura's brows arched. "A thousand acres is small?"

"Here in Texas is it," George said with a laugh. "Some ranches are four and five times bigger than that."

"There's so much empty land here," May put in. "Not at all like Michigan. It's beautiful."

George nodded. "I can't imagine living in a city again."

Laura wasn't surprised, and said so.

"But out here, there really isn't much to see," he told them. "There's a river over the rise as well as a small creek a couple hundred yards in that direction." He pointed away from the house. "When the house was first built, there was no well so they had to fetch water from there."

"That must have been difficult in the winter," Laura commented.

"It rarely gets cold enough here to freeze, though, so there was always enough."

"The tools are kept in there," he said as they passed a small wooden building, "so if you want garden tools or…I can't think of anything else you'd need in there, but if you do, that's where you'll find them."

Soon they stopped at one of the corrals where a large black horse with a white blaze and socks was grazing. As they approached, the horse looked up at them, and apparently deciding they weren't worth paying attention to, returned to his meal.

"We're starting a breeding program next year," George said, smiling as he rested his gaze on the horse. "I just bought this stallion and he's going to be breeding the mares in the other corral come spring."

Laura felt heat rise in her cheeks. It seemed strange that it was acceptable to talk about such things to a woman here in the west. "He's magnificent."

George laughed. "There's no need to whisper."

She realized she'd lowered her voice so she didn't disturb the horse and joined him, laughing.

Turning to laugh with May, she realized she'd been so entranced with the horse that she hadn't notice May wandering off. Scanning the area, she saw her back at the corral where she'd watched the man working with the cream-colored horse earlier. Now there were four horses in the corral.

Taking Laura's elbow, George led her to the corral where May was standing. The heat from his hand seeped through the thin fabric of her dress and sent tingles shooting up her arm. Not only her arm but her entire body tingled at his touch.

The strange sensation made her breath catch in her throat.

He glanced at her curiously, his brows in a frown.

She forced a smile, although the reaction to his touch was so confusing it frightened her a little.

Releasing Laura when they reached the corral, he leaned his elbows on the top rail of the fence and rested one booted foot on the bottom rail.

He held out his hand, and immediately, a reddish-brown horse moved toward him and stopped inches from his hand. "Watch," George said, grinning.

He didn't move, and seconds later, the horse shook his head, let out a noise that sounded like some kind of snort and nudged his hand.

George's expression softened and he gently ran his hand down the horse's face and scratched a spot on its forehead. "This is Nero. He's my horse. Do you ladies know how to ride?"

Laura shook her head. "We did have horses, but I had nothing to do with them. They were for pulling the carriage."

"I learned how to ride when I was a child but I haven't ridden since," May said.

Laura and May moved to stand beside George.

"He's beautiful," Laura said, entranced by the bond between the man and the animal.

She caught a movement out of the corner of her eye and turned to see a giant of a man walking toward them.

"Afternoon, boss." The man stopped beside George and tipped his hat in Laura and May's direction. "Ladies."

"Laura Shelton," George said, his gaze settling on Laura. "May Deline," he added, nodding at May, "this is Dutch Vanfleet, the ranch foreman and my right arm. This place would fall apart without him."

"It's nice to meet you," Laura said, smiling an acknowledgement.

May held out her hand. "It's a pleasure," she said.

Dutch took her hand, burying it in his and holding it a second or two longer than necessary. "It's my pleasure."

Laura gazed at Dutch and May. The way he was gazing at May…he liked what he saw. And it looked like May felt the same way.

"Where's Alice?" George asked Dutch.

As if he'd forgotten they were there, Dutch pulled his hand away from May. "Oh…uh…she went riding with Bobby. She's been doing so well with her lessons that he thought she was ready to try riding a trail rather than just in the corral."

"Is she riding Sunny?"

Dutch nodded.

Turning to Laura and May, George explained. "Sunny is Alice's horse. In fact, Alice was there when Sunny was born and gave her the name. She was likely too young to remember it, though."

Life was certainly different out here in the west, Laura thought. While she'd been protected from anything considered unseemly or dangerous for a child, here, small children were exposed to experiences she'd still never taken part in.

"Sunny is still young, not full grown enough for an adult's weight," George went on, "but we figure even when she's full grown, she likely won't grow too big for Alice to handle."

Suddenly, as if Dutch had conjured them up, two figures on horseback appeared from within a stand of trees.

Laura was surprised to see such a small child seated on such a large animal, but the little girl seemed to be in complete control and was comfortable riding.

While they watched, Bobby and Alice closed the gap and drew the horses to a stop beside them.

Laura's heart melted when she got a close look at George's daughter, soon to be her daughter. So small, with blonde hair tied back in a pigtail and bright blue eyes. She was adorable. She didn't look happy, though, and Laura couldn't help wondering why.

Bobby, the young man with curly black hair and eyes so dark they looked almost black, smiled and nodded a greeting from where he was astride a brown-and-white dappled horse. "Afternoon," he said.

He dismounted and before he had a chance to help Alice, she swung her leg over the saddle and slid off. He barely caught her before she tumbled onto the ground.

"I'll take care of the horses," Bobby said.

"Thanks," George said, then turned his attention to his daughter while Bobby led the two horses to the barn.

"Did you have a nice ride?" he asked.

Alice nodded at her father, revealing dimples and a gap where a tooth used to be. "We went through the trees to where the river is. I wanted to look for frogs but Bobby said no and made me come home."

"So what happened to your dress?" he asked, shaking his head in resignation. "Didn't you promise me before I left that you'd stay clean and tidy for Miss Shelton?"

Laura could tell by the tone of his voice that he wasn't angry, just frustrated. From what he'd told them on the way to town, Alice wasn't like most little girls. She didn't play with dolls and have imaginary tea parties. She liked frogs and worms, and climbing trees and digging for buried treasure.

"If you haven't already guessed, this is my daughter, Alice," George said, taking the little girl's hand in his and drawing her close.

Alice took a step toward Laura. "Papa said I should stay clean 'til we got you, but there was some pretty flowers I wanted to get for you and they was near some bushes and I tripped and the grass got me dirty and the flowers got broken." She held up one foot. "And I got mud on my shoes. Sorry."

Laura was surprised that a child that small could say everything Alice had said without even stopping to take a breath. She crouched to Alice's eye level and smiled at her. "There's no need to be sorry, Alice," she said softly. "I like to pick flowers, too, and sometimes I even get dirty." Her heart went out to Alice, a memory of doing almost the same thing when she was that age. She had been punished, and she'd never forgotten it.

"You do?" Alice asked, her eyes widening.

Laura nodded.

"I do, but I do try to stay clean. Maybe we'll both

have to be very careful in the future if we're picking flowers."

"Okay." Alice's gaze whipped in her father's direction and she grinned. "Is she going to be my new mama?"

Laura met George's gaze. He was smiling at her, yet there was something more in his eyes. Something she couldn't define, but that made her skin tingle and her heart flutter. Suddenly, she felt something grazing her skin. She looked down to see Alice's hand wrapped around three of her fingers. "You want to come see Sunny?"

What was she supposed to do? She cut a glance at George, and getting no guidance from him, smiled down at Alice. "I'd love to."

CHAPTER 9

George looked on as Laura and Alice crossed the yard and disappeared into the barn. Alice was looking up at Laura, smiling, their hands still clasped together. He'd been worried about Alice accepting another woman as her mother, but it seemed he'd been concerned about nothing.

"If you want to go with them…" Dutch's voice filtered into George's thoughts.

"What…? Oh…" George said, realizing Dutch was speaking to him.

Dutch nodded in the direction of the barn. "I'm happy to keep Miss Deline company," he said, smiling down at May. "If she doesn't object, that is."

May returned his smile. "I don't object at all."

Was something starting between his foreman and his bride's best friend? It looked that way to George as he muttered something about not being gone long and following Laura and Alice into the barn.

He paused to let his eyes adjust to the dim light inside, Alice's voice carrying through the still air from the stall at the back of the barn. "Don't be scared," he heard her say. "Here, you take the brush like this…"

A few seconds later, he heard a laugh. Laura's laugh and then Alice's a moment later. The sweetest sounds he'd ever heard.

For the first time since he'd walked into the Blue Sapphire and asked for Miranda's help, George felt as if he'd made the right decision.

Hurrying to the rear of the barn, he stopped just outside the stall. There, inside, was Sunny, nuzzling Laura's head. Her feathery hat had slipped and her hair had loosened from the hairpins, tumbling in curls around her shoulders.

Desire slammed into him. Desire he could not—would not—act on. He needed a housekeeper, a mother for Alice. Nothing else.

Supper was finished, the dishes and the kitchen cleaned up, and Laura and May were sitting on the settee in the main room. George was upstairs settling Alice for the night and this was the first chance Laura had had to talk to her best friend in private.

"He told me he doesn't want love," Laura whispered in case George happened to be within earshot. He likely wouldn't be happy to hear her speaking about him behind his back.

May gave her a sympathetic smile. "That's a shame," she said, "but did you really expect him to? Surely spending your life with him will still be better than with Linus or one of the other old men your father had in mind. Do you think any of them were in love with you, or were they in love with your dowry?"

"I suppose that's true." Laura let out a sigh. "I admit I did hope we'd fall in love like in the books, just like Elizabeth and Mr. Darcy."

"You just met," May reminded her. "Most people don't fall in love at first sight. Are you starting to have feelings for him?" May asked, then chuckled. "Not that I'd blame you. He's handsome and very nice."

"He is, but he's made it clear that he only wants a housekeeper, and a mother for Alice." Laura got up and crossed to the window. Outside, the sun was resting on the horizon, casting ribbons of gold and red and pink across the sky. She'd never really paid much attention to sunsets in Springhill. With so many houses in the way and the smoke from the factories, she'd paid no heed to them. But during her journey to Texas and now that she was here in Sapphire Springs with nothing between her and the horizon but emptiness, she was entranced by them.

She squinted into the deepening shadows at movement near the bunkhouse until she recognized Dutch heading toward them. "The foreman is coming to see George," she said. "I should go and tell him."

Before she reached the bottom of the stairs, a knock came to the door. She opened it and smiled.

"Good evening," she said. "George is upstairs, so I'll go—"

Dutch took off his hat, holding it by the brim in both hands. "Uh…no…I don't need to see him," he said.

He cast a glance into the main room, his gaze settling on May. A tiny burst of amusement filled Laura. The foreman was here to see May. "I have something on the stove, so if you'll excuse me…"

She turned away, grinning at May as she passed by on her way to the kitchen. Once there, she paused, listening.

"Uh…Miss…I was wondering…that is, if you're not busy, would you want to take a short walk with me?"

Laura heard the rustle of May's skirts and her footsteps on the floor as she got up and crossed the room. "You can call me May," she said softly, "and I'd be delighted to take a walk with you."

The door opened and closed a few seconds later, and she smiled. At least one of them might find love in Texas.

George tiptoed down the stairs. Alice was finally asleep, after two bedtime stories, a glass of water and a promise to let her go riding after the wedding if she didn't get dirty before they left for the church the next day.

He was surprised to find Laura alone, but in a way, he was pleased. He wanted to spend time with her, especially when they had a few minutes to themselves. "Where's May?" he asked, joining her on the settee.

"She went for a stroll with Dutch," Laura told him.

George wasn't sure how he felt about that. He had no designs on May, but he knew his foreman, and he'd left more than one broken heart behind him. He didn't like to think that Laura's best friend could be next. "Oh."

The tone of his voice must have given away his concern, because Laura gave him a curious glance. "Is something wrong?"

He shook his head. "No, not really, but…I hope she doesn't read anything into it. Dutch isn't the marrying kind, and I'd hate to see her get hurt."

"I hope so, too," Laura said, lifting her hand to her mouth to try to hide a yawn.

George saw it and got up. "It's getting late," he said, holding out his hand. "Come on. I'll show you to your room and you can get some sleep."

For a second or two, she stared at his hand and he wondered if she was willing to share a little contact. Then she looked up at him, smiled sweetly and rested her hand in his.

Her skin was like satin against his, and that same sensation he'd felt before rushed through him. His breath caught as the realization came that if the touch of her hand caused such a reaction, having her in his bed would create an inferno.

Releasing her quickly, he led the way up the stairs, and then pointed out Alice's bedroom and the bedrooms May and Laura could use. "Until the wedding," he amended when he opened the door to the bedroom beside his.

Her cheeks reddened and she avoided his gaze.

Should he mention that he'd decided at some point during the afternoon that he'd like to have a real marriage? He didn't know. It was something he'd never thought to ask John Weaver or any of the other men he knew who'd brought mail-order brides to town. How had they handled the wedding night?

He wanted Laura. Wanted to kiss her, to touch her, to make her his in every way. He just didn't love her. He had the right to do what he wanted with her, but he couldn't bring himself to force her to give in to him. She was no saloon whore, but would taking her to bed be like treating her like one because love wasn't involved?

Laura's voice burst into his discussion with himself and took the question out of his hands. She met his gaze, her face flushed. "Do you expect...?" she asked in a quivering voice.

He didn't want her to feel as if she had to perform her marital duty. "I want to be honest with you. I do want to have a real marriage, and maybe more children one day, but if you aren't willing..."

"I...I'm not sure..."

He nodded. "Then we'll wait until you are, but I would like you to share my bed."

She moved away from him and stepped into the bedroom. She didn't answer for quite some time, just stood and stared at the bed.

When he'd almost given up on getting an answer, she turned and faced him. "Yes," she said, "I can do that."

Dawn was peeking through a gap in the curtains when Laura woke the next morning. It took her a few seconds to remember where she was and what day it was. Her wedding day.

In the dimly lit room, she could make out a bureau holding a china jug and basin on the wall facing the bed. Near the window was a chair and a small table where she could sit and watch the cattle roaming the fields in the distance. And in the corner, a large wardrobe where her wedding dress hung.

She'd lain awake for a long time after George left her the night before, her thoughts spinning wildly.

George wanted to have his way with her, and she had to admit the thought both excited and terrified her. She'd overheard two of the maids talking once when they didn't know she was listening, and she'd been intrigued when they'd described what happened between a man and a woman, that it was exciting and like fireworks. The strangest thing was, before she'd overheard that conversation between the maids, she'd heard from a married friend that the act was painful, embarrassing and something to endure rather than enjoy. She couldn't help being curious which was true.

She already found George so handsome and considerate, so surely that would help. And whenever he'd touched her or taken her hand, strange sensations had fluttered through her and she'd grown warm even though the temperature hadn't changed.

She had no idea what those feelings meant, but letting him do…*that*…to her had to be better than allowing a man like Linus to bed her. And she was sure she wouldn't have a choice if she married any of the men her father had chosen for her before she left.

She still hadn't decided what to do by the time exhaustion finally overtook her.

It's so early, she thought, but George had explained that the day started at dawn on the ranch. She snuggled down for a few more seconds, then forced herself to get out of bed.

Clattering from downstairs reached her ears. She quickly dressed, gave her hair a quick brush and headed toward the noise.

May was cracking eggs into a pottery bowl in the kitchen when Laura went in. Alice was sitting at the table drawing.

"Good morning," May said when she entered the kitchen. "I've started breakfast. George is already out doing morning chores."

Guilt washed over Laura. She was the one who

should be preparing breakfast for George and Alice, not May. And one day soon, she would, as soon as she learned how. "I'm so sorry. I didn't sleep well at all last night."

"Did you have bad dreams?" Alice asked. "I sometimes have bad dreams and Papa holds my hand until I go back to sleep. Tell Papa if you have bad dreams and he can hold your hand, too."

The mention of George holding her hand brought back the memory of those strange feelings that had surged through her.

"Okay?"

Alice's voice penetrated her thoughts. "What… oh…yes, I will."

The little girl went back to her drawing, satisfied that she'd solved Laura's problem. If only…

Laura moved to stand beside May.

"I'm not surprised," May whispered, smiling. "I'm sure you're nervous like any other bride would be."

Laura nodded. "Terrified, actually," she said with a small smile, "but I don't want to think about that now. I need to learn to make breakfast. What can I do to help?"

May took a fork out of the drawer and handed it to Laura. "Coffee's made, bacon is cooking. Why don't you do the eggs?"

"What exactly am I supposed to do with the eggs?" Laura asked.

"Whip them, like this," May told her, taking a fork out of the drawer and demonstrating the technique.

Laura took the fork from her. It took a few attempts to move her hands the way May had showed her, and much of the egg was splattered on the table, but finally, she got it. "I did it," she said, her pride in her accomplishment showing in her voice.

"You did," May agreed. "See, you'll be a great cook in no time."

Laura chuckled. She wasn't sure she agreed with May, but it was a goal.

At that moment, the door opened and George walked in.

"Breakfast is almost ready," May told him, "and Laura is doing the eggs."

He gave her an encouraging smile, and her heart swelled. What was it about this man—this stranger, really—that made her want to please him just so he'd smile at her that way?

George's stomach was in knots and his chest was so tight he could barely draw a deep breath. He stood beside the wagon in front of the house waiting for Laura, May and Alice to come out. George would take Laura to town, while Dutch, in another wagon behind him, would take May and Alice.

Finally, the door opened and they came out, May and Alice first, and then Laura. George's breath caught. He'd never seen a more beautiful woman.

She was wearing a pale blue silk dress decorated

with lace and ribbons that left her neck bare. Her hair was piled high on her head, tiny white flowers tucked into the curls. And in her hands, she was carrying white flowers tied with blue ribbon.

She and Alice had disappeared that morning, refusing to tell him where they were going. They must have gone to pick flowers.

She was downright beautiful.

As she approached, he noticed her face was flushed and her hands were trembling. He was shaking on the inside, but at least it didn't show. He was glad about that.

A few minutes later, they were on their way. She was quiet, her hands wrapped around the flowers in her lap.

"Are you nervous?" he asked finally.

She nodded. "I suppose you aren't, since you've done this before."

"I am." He had done this before, but he couldn't remember ever being this nervous, not even when he'd married Verna. Of course, back then he'd been in love. So much in love he couldn't think straight.

This time was different. He wanted Laura in his bed, but love wasn't part of the arrangement. He did like her, though. And if the short time he'd known her was any indication, in time he could like her a lot. He wasn't sure how he felt about that.

George's throat was parched by the time he and

Laura arrived at the pastor's house in town. He climbed out of the wagon and tied the horses to the hitching post in front of the house. Then he reached up, gripped Laura around her waist and lifted her out of the wagon. Her rosewater scent wafted over him and her hair tickled his cheek as her soft curves grazed his chest.

He couldn't resist. He held her a few seconds longer than he needed to, the temptation to kiss her almost more than he could stand. And the worst of it was, he sensed she wouldn't resist, that maybe she wanted him to kiss her, too.

"Everything okay here?" Dutch's voice was enough to break the spell of the moment.

George quickly released Laura and waited for Dutch, May and Alice to reach them. Surprisingly enough, Alice's dress was still clean.

"Everything's fine," he replied. Turning to Laura, he gave her an encouraging smile. "Ready?"

CHAPTER 10

Laura stood beside George in front of the fireplace in the pastor's house a few minutes later. May stood beside her, holding the small bouquet of wildflowers for her, while Dutch and Alice stood beside George.

Her knees threatened to buckle and her fingers trembled as George took her hand in his and slid the wedding band onto her finger while Reverend Ford said the words that would join her and George forever. Yet, when she looked up at George and met his dark grayish-blue gaze, all she felt was happiness.

"I now pronounce you man and wife." The pastor smiled at them both.

Her heart skipped a beat. She was a now a married woman. A wife. And a mother. And even though they didn't love each other and there was no reason to think they ever would, there was no reason they couldn't be happy together. And she was going to do everything she could to be a good wife and mother so that he never regretted this day.

"You can kiss Laura now, George," she heard the pastor say, but all she could do was gaze at this man, this incredibly handsome man who was now her husband.

He looked down at her, his dark eyes boring into hers. Yet there was something else in that gaze. Desire. She'd seen it in men's eyes before, and recognized it now.

He didn't love her, but he wanted her, and that knowledge warmed her. Cupping her chin in his work-roughened hands, he lowered his lips to hers, grazing them gently, and sending sparks of heat to every cell of her body. The sensation was indescribable, and…wondrous.

The kiss was over before her brain could register it, yet even after he pulled away, that heat refused to leave her. Heavens, she thought, if a mere brushing of his lips against hers could cause such incredible sensations, would she even survive their wedding night?

"Congratulations," May said, enveloping her in a hug. "I'm so happy for you."

"What…oh…yes, thank you…"

Alice tugged at her dress. "Papa says you're my mama now that you had a wedding."

Laura crouched until they were the same height. "I am," she said, smiling. From the moment she'd seen Alice, dirt and all, she'd fallen in love with the little girl. She couldn't imagine loving her own child more than she already loved Alice. She nodded. "Is that all right with you?"

"Will you bake cookies?"

Laura pressed her lips together to stop herself from smiling. Obviously the little girl had priorities. "I will."

"Will you tuck me into bed and read me stories?"

"I'll do that too."

"Will you look for frogs and worms with me?"

Laura hesitated at that question, then nodded and smiled. "Not all the time, but maybe once in a while. So, what do you think? Can I be your mama now?"

Alice grinned and took Laura's hand, fingering the new wedding band on her finger. Then she nodded, and Laura's heart swelled.

A few minutes later, after accepting congratulations from the pastor and his wife and extracting a promise to come to the service on Sunday, they all went back outside. George helped Laura back into the wagon while Dutch, May and Alice got into the other wagon.

George flicked the reins and they headed back toward the ranch

For a few minutes, Laura was lost in her own thoughts, but when she looked back to check on the others who were supposed to be traveling right behind them, the trail was empty.

Her forehead creased in a frown, and she laid her hand on George's arm. "Where are Dutch, and May and Alice?"

George shifted and smiled at her. "Dutch is taking them to the hotel in town."

"What? Why?"

"It's our wedding day," he said.

As if he had to remind her, Laura thought.

"May thought we might like to spend it together, so she offered to take care of Alice overnight. Dutch is going to take care of the chores, and while we were at the Fords' house, Miranda took a wedding supper out to the house."

What? They were going to be alone in the house all night? Laura's heartbeat raced and she felt the blood drain from her face, leaving her short of breath and a little light-headed, yet she couldn't say why. George had never been anything but kind and considerate, so she had no reason to be concerned about being alone with him, and yet she was.

She'd been curious about the goings-on between men and women, but now that the time was almost near that she'd find out the truth, she had to admit she was afraid.

"Are you all right?" George asked, concern in his gaze. "You look pale. You aren't sick, are you?"

She shook her head. "No," she said, noticing her voice was even a little shaky. "I'm fine." She tried to smile, but when he didn't smile back, she knew she'd failed.

He drew the wagon to a halt. "Are you sure? Do I need to take you back to town to the doctor?"

She was being ridiculous, she told herself. She was

a married woman now and she had a duty to perform. And if what was about to happen really was like the fireworks the maid had described, she had nothing to fear and everything to gain. And enjoy.

She smiled again. This time it was genuine. "I'm fine. Really. Except for one thing."

"What's that?" Again, his voice was filled with concern.

She laughed. "I'm starving."

"Are you sad that your family wasn't here today," George asked later that night once they'd finished supper and were sitting on the front porch. The air had cooled, and a soft breeze whispered in the trees. Light from the lamp in the house spilled through the window, casting the porch in golden shadow.

"A little," Laura replied honestly, "but they would never have approved of our marriage, so it's best that they weren't here. I did have May with me, and she's the sister I never had."

"Tell me about your life back in Michigan," he said. "I assume your family isn't poor."

She chuckled. "No, my family is definitely not poor. I'm not sure exactly what my father does, but something to do with mining. He always said a woman didn't need to know about business."

"Do you have brothers and sisters?"

"Yes," she replied. "I have two sisters, but they're

both married now. I think that's why my father was so determined that whoever I married would already be established financially since he'd control my inheritance one day. I think he's disinherited me now, though."

George took her hand, that now-familiar warmth spreading through her and settling low in her belly. "It doesn't matter," he said. "We might never be wealthy, but we'll have enough to support us and I'll make sure you never have to worry about money."

She felt a yawn coming on, and even though she tried to hide it, George saw it. "It's getting late. We should go inside and get some sleep."

"All right."

On shaking legs, she went inside and up the stairs to the bedroom she'd now be sharing with her husband. George followed, lighting the lamp on the table beside the bed. "I'll leave you to get ready for bed," he said, then smiled and left the room.

Laura's fingers were all thumbs as she tried to unbutton her dress and untie her corsets. Finally, she slipped into the white silk nightdress she'd brought with her. It was soft, and gathered at the neck with a ribbon.

She gazed at the bed, but couldn't bring herself to get into it to wait for George.

Instead, she stood in the corner of the room. Why, she couldn't say, but for some reason, she needed to be as far away from the bed as possible.

She wasn't waiting long before she heard George's

boots on the stairs and a few seconds later, he came into the room.

He stood at the doorway for what seemed an eternity, not speaking, just looking at her. Finally, he smiled. "You look like you're about to be mauled by an angry bear."

"What?" Her voice was weak, barely squeaking past the dryness in her throat.

He crossed the room, sat down on the edge of the bed and pulled off his boots. Then he unbuttoned his shirt and threw it onto the chair.

Laura had never seen a man's bare chest before, and the play of muscles beneath his skin with every movement fascinated her. She had a sudden urge to touch them, and her face flamed at the direction of her shameful thoughts.

He came to stand in front of her, so close his unique scent reached her nose.

"If you don't want to have a real marriage, all you have to do is tell me," he said.

"I..." she began. What did she want? Then the words came out of her mouth of their own accord and she realized she really did want a real marriage. She wanted to know what happened between men and women, and there was only one way to find out. "I do, I'm just..."

"There's no reason to be scared," he said softly, taking both her hands in his. "Why don't we start with a kiss, and whenever you want to stop, all you have to do is tell me and we'll stop. Okay?"

She swallowed thickly and nodded. Her heart was beating furiously as he released her hands and closed the gap between them.

His eyes had darkened, shining with what she now recognized as desire as he cradled her face in his hands and looked down at her, his gaze searing her soul.

Her breath left her as he lowered his mouth to hers, brushing her lips gently with his.

The world faded, and her heart beat furiously in her chest. Too soon, the kiss was over, and he stood back, smiling down at her. "Again?"

Her brain had shut down, and she couldn't speak, so she just nodded. This time, he wrapped his arms around her waist, drawing her toward him. The pressure of his body against hers did something to her senses, and she was unable to think, to do anything other than just feel.

Again, his lips lightly brushed hers, but then his hands threaded into her hair and the kiss deepened. Something inside her changed, and she wanted to stay there, wrapped in his arms forever.

Then his lips left her mouth and trailed a row of kisses down her jaw to the curve of her neck, leaving a burning trail in its wake. He reached up to the neckline of her nightdress and loosened the ribbon, giving him access to her shoulder.

Her skin was on fire, her breathing ragged, and something was happening to her that she didn't understand. All she knew was that she was willing… no, eager…to quench the need building inside her.

When he lifted his head to look into her eyes, she saw her own feelings mirrored in his.

"Do you want to keep going?" he asked, his breath tickling her cheek.

She wanted that more than she wanted her next breath. She nodded. "Yes please."

CHAPTER 11

George opened the door the next morning after doing his morning chores. He'd left Laura asleep in their bed, and it had been one of the hardest things he'd ever done.

The temptation to wrap his arms around her and wake her with a kiss—and more—had been almost more than he could stand.

He paused inside the doorway, looking at her. She hadn't heard him come in, and she was sitting at the table, her head in her hands, a crumpled handkerchief at her elbow.

Something was very wrong. "Laura?"

At the sound of his voice, her head jerked up and she let out a tiny squeak as she looked up at him, her hands scrubbing at her tear-filled eyes.

Hurrying to her, he crouched beside the chair and wrapped his arms around her. "Laura? What's wrong?"

She blinked, her lashes spiked with tears, and in a wobbly voice, she said, "I burned the eggs."

"What?" He rose to his full height and crossed to the stove. Sure enough, a clump of brownish black eggs was stuck to the bottom and sides of the skillet.

"I'm sorry," she said, coming to stand beside him. "I tried to——"

Her cheeks were flushed, her eyes puffy and red, and yet he still found her to be one of the most beautiful women he'd ever seen. He couldn't resist her. He leaned in, kissed her soundly and wrapped his arms around her. When he lifted his mouth from hers, he met her gaze. "This was the first time you've tried to cook yourself, and maybe it didn't turn out well, but it shouldn't bring you to tears."

"I wanted to make you breakfast and…I failed and now you won't have anything to eat…"

He was surprised she was so upset, and he didn't know how to make her feel better. "You can try again tomorrow. May will be here and she can guide you if you need it, but I bet you'll do much better next time."

She nodded, her chin quivering but without tears now.

"I'll tell you what," he went on. "Why don't we go into town now. We'll have breakfast at the Blue Sapphire and you can meet Miranda and John and when we're done, we'll get May and Alice and bring them home."

"What about breakfast for them? Shouldn't they come with us?"

George shook his head. "I arranged for them to have breakfast in the hotel because I thought we'd be getting them after lunch, but…"

Laura nodded and her chin quivered again. She was still upset about burning the eggs, and he hated seeing that defeated look in her eyes. "But I'm looking forward to showing you around town."

She gave him a watery smile. "I'd like that."

"Good." He pulled a clean handkerchief out of his pocket and gently dabbed at her eyes. "Now, no more tears. Go and get ready and I'll hitch up the wagon."

She nodded and hurried out.

He watched her go, his stomach settling. He'd thought something serious had happened, and he'd been surprised to find her so upset over a few eggs. Had she been worried that he'd be angry? Or that he'd criticize her?

His mind drifted back to the night before. She'd been so afraid, but at the same time, she'd trusted him to be gentle with her, and she'd given herself to him even though he'd given her the chance to stop several times.

That she'd offered herself to him so freely and trusted him so completely did something to his insides. It made him feel…happy, a feeling he hadn't had for a long time.

And if he was never the cause of tears in Laura's eyes again, that would make him happier still.

⁓

Laura sat quietly in the wagon on the way to town. She felt…awkward. Now that she'd gotten over her cooking failure, she had time to process what had happened between them the night before.

She slid a glance at George, doing her best to hide the fact that she was looking at him. A muscled chest that had pressed against her. Strong arms that her wrapped around her. Hands and fingers that had touched her intimately.

Her veins tingled at the memory and that now-familiar fluttering sensation stirred in her stomach.

"What?"

She'd been so caught up in her own thoughts she hadn't realized he'd noticed her staring at him.

"Nothing," she lied.

"Are you feeling all right this morning? After…"

Her cheeks burned. "Oh…" she murmured, turning her head away. She couldn't bear to meet his gaze, knowing exactly what he was referring to.

"Laura," he said softly. "Look at me."

When she didn't respond, he drew the wagon to a halt. "Laura!" His hands gripped her shoulders and turned her to face him.

"For this to work, we need to be able to talk," he said, hooking a finger under her chin and forcing her to look up at him. "I don't want you to be too embarrassed or afraid to tell me anything. Okay?"

She nodded, but said nothing.

"What happened between us last night was… special, and exciting, and amazing. It probably wasn't for you since it was your first time, but trust me, it'll be better next time."

Laura's eyes widened. It wasn't possible to be better than the night before. Was it? She couldn't wait to find out.

He leaned closer, took her hands in his. Her breathing quickened, remembering how those hands had changed her life. Then he kissed her gently, sweetly. "You know," he said when he drew back, "I think you and I are going to have a very good life together."

The diner was busy when George opened the door and ushered Laura inside. The aroma of freshly baked bread, bacon and beef roasting mingled in the air, made her mouth water and her stomach rumble.

Only two tables were empty, both at the far wall. At least the town had one thing in common with Springhill, Laura mused. Everyone seemed to know everyone else. Her head was spinning with names by the time they managed to weave their way through the tables and introductions were finished.

Laura dropped into a chair and chuckled. "People here like to talk, don't they?"

"They do," George said. "Out here, a lot of us don't see each other much, so when we do get together, we tend to talk a lot to catch up on the latest news."

Laura nodded. "That's understandable. Back home, it seems all we do is socialize, especially the women. Afternoon tea, luncheons, meetings of the charities we support. We're busy all the time."

"I hope you won't miss it much, because that's not how things are here."

"I won't." While she knew there would be some things she'd miss about her life of leisure in Springhill, she'd always disliked the constant gossip, the way the women judged each other behind their backs while they complimented and praised each other to their faces.

Just then, a young woman approached, a coffeepot in her hand. Two mugs were already upside down on the table. "Morning, George."

"Morning, Miranda," George said, then introduced Laura.

"I'm sorry I can't sit and chat with you right now," Miranda said, "but I'm happy to meet you. Since I was a mail-order bride, I know how hard it is to settle out here with a man you don't know, so we should get together sometime and I can answer any questions you have or offer you some advice if you want it."

Laura smiled. "I'd love that," she replied.

A deep voice called Miranda's name. She waved an acknowledgement to the man and raised the coffee pot. "Coffee?"

Both Laura and George nodded. Miranda turned the mugs right side up and filled them. "The menu's on the board," she told them. "Give me a shout when you're ready to order."

Then she hurried away.

"I hope you and Miranda will become friends," George said, watching Miranda leave.

Laura followed his gaze. "I hope so, too."

CHAPTER 12

"I really like him." May stopped rolling the pastry for the apple pie she and Laura were making a few days later and stared into space. "He's so handsome, and nice, don't you think?"

Laura's eyes widened. May did not fall in love easily, but it did seem that after her walk with Dutch, she was smitten.

"Dutch is a nice man," Alice put in from where she was sitting at the other end of the table with a lump of pastry, patting it into a circle the way May had showed her. "He plays with me a lot."

Laura finished slicing the last apple and put the slices in the bowl beside her. "He does seem nice, but I only spoke to him for a few minutes. Now what do I do with the apples?"

May chuckled. "Oh…yes…the apples," she said. "My mind was off somewhere."

"With Dutch, I'd guess," Laura teased.

May nodded, her cheeks turning pink. "They're ready to go into the crust once I finish rolling it out." Quickly, she gave the pastry a few last rolls and then set it in the pie plate. "He asked me to go into town with him tomorrow evening for supper. Do you think I should go?"

"Of course you should go, if you want to," Laura said, carefully spreading the apples on top of the pastry. She left a few slices for Alice's pastry and while she looked on, May showed Alice how to pull the edges of the pastry together to make a ball with the apples inside.

"I do want to…" May said, going back to her place at the table and starting to roll the last ball of pastry for the top of the pie.

"Then what's the problem?"

"It's just…" May began. "If he wants to court me, wouldn't that be awkward if it doesn't work out with both of us living here?"

Laura wiped her hands on a towel and faced her friend. "It's only supper," she said. "And maybe it will work out and you and Dutch will get married."

Alice grinned. "Is there gonna be another wedding?"

Laura and May both realized at the same time that they needed to be careful what they said within earshot of Alice. "Nooo," they said simultaneously. "There is not going to be a wedding."

"Awww," Alice complained. "I like weddings."

"No more talk of weddings, okay?" Laura insisted.

"Okay," Alice muttered, then went back to arranging the pastry around the apples, weddings forgotten, at least for the moment.

May giggled and whispered in Laura's ear. "It would be wonderful if that happened, though, wouldn't it?"

Laura joined her laughter. "It really would."

Just then, George walked into the kitchen. Laura's pulse quickened the way it seemed to every time she looked at him now.

"What are my three favorite ladies up to?" he asked, his gaze settling on Alice.

Alice stood up on her chair. "Look, Papa," she said as she gathered up the ball she'd made. "We're making pies."

"So I see," he said, smiling. "And I bet they'll be the tastiest pies ever."

He met Laura's gaze, his eyes crinkling at the corners in a smile, and gave her a slight nod.

Laura smiled back. He was pleased, and that pleased her.

"That was a great meal, May," George said, resting against the back of his chair after supper that night.

May stood up and started collecting the dirty dishes. "Thanks, George, but Laura made it all except the pies. I told her what to do, but she did everything herself."

Turning his head to speak to Laura, he grinned. "You're a fast learner." He'd discovered she was a fast learner and eager student with other things besides cooking, too, and he couldn't wait to give her another lesson.

He expected her to blush, but instead, she met his gaze. "I'm always willing to learn new skills."

Luckily, May had disappeared into the kitchen with Alice. Heat and desire swept through George. He'd thought he could tease her, but apparently she could play his game, and play it well. Not one to be outdone, he grinned. "Practice makes perfect."

"So I hear. I'm always willing to practice so I can improve."

She was flirting with him! He was curious to see how far Laura would take their little wordplay and about to say something even more risqué but May appeared in the doorway, Alice in front of her carrying a small pitcher of milk. May had her hands at the ready in case the pitcher was too heavy, but the determination on Alice's face told George she'd never admit she wasn't strong enough to carry it.

"Then you can learn how to make dumplings tomorrow?" she said to Laura.

"What…? Oh…of course…" Laura said. "I'm going to be exhausted with all this learning I'm doing," she added with a smile and a quick glance in George's direction.

"Then why don't you and George go and relax

while Alice and I finish cleaning up. You'll help me, won't you, Alice?"

Alice looked up at her father, the question in her eyes. "Just this time you can stay up past bedtime."

"I'll help," Alice said to May. "After my milk."

"Are you sure?" Laura asked. "I don't mind—"

May waved away her objection. "Go."

What had gotten into her? Laura wondered as she stepped out onto the porch with George. She'd been…what was it her mother called it—coquettish—with men before, but never like this. Flirting had always been fun, but tonight, with George, there had been an undercurrent, a deeper meaning to their words.

As they'd talked, a fluttering had begun in her stomach, spreading through her as his double meanings to what he said became increasingly clear. She could have stopped him, but she found their little game exciting, and anticipation of the night ahead bubbled up inside her.

The sun had almost set. Only a few rays of golden light still hovered at the horizon. The scent of pine was heavy in the air, and the faint sounds of birds in the trees broke the silence.

"I like to be out here and watch the sun go down but I often don't have time," George said quietly, taking her hand in his. His thumb moved over her palm, sending a thrill up her arm.

Laura nodded, then realizing he couldn't see her, said, "I'm not surprised. It's beautiful."

"You have no idea how happy it made me to see Alice with you and May in the kitchen. I just know that with your help, she'll grow into a woman who has poise and manners and…just like you."

Laura chuckled. "Are you sure you want her to be like me? I know how to host a tea party, how to dance and play croquet, but none of those things are very useful out here. I don't know how to cook, or clean, or do laundry. I can be stubborn, and overly sensitive and sometimes, I don't act like a lady at all."

The sound of the laughter that erupted from him warmed her. It was a contagious laugh, and moments later, she found herself laughing, too.

"I'm glad you came," he said a minute or so later. "Not only for Alice's sake, but for mine, too. I didn't realize how much I missed having company in the house in the evenings."

Her heart swelled. She turned to meet his eyes, so dark now that she could barely see him other than in shadow, yet she didn't need to. She'd memorized every detail of his face. She smiled, even though she knew he couldn't see it. "I'm glad I came, too."

During the next few weeks, Laura learned to cook and bake as well as take care of the house. She spent as much time as she could with Alice, and the first time Alice hugged her and wanted a goodnight kiss, Laura's heart felt as if it might explode with love for the little girl.

May spent most evenings with Dutch, either in town or just strolling outdoors, which left Laura alone with George after Alice was asleep. They read, or played checkers, or just talked, and every day, she fell more and more in love with her husband.

George seemed happy, especially when Alice started trying to copy everything Laura was doing. The little girl still liked to spend time with the ranch hands, and especially in the stable or riding Sunny, but she spent less and less time digging for buried treasure, looking for worms, and climbing the tallest oak tree in the yard, which Laura knew pleased George.

But did George have any feelings for her? She didn't know. He was always kind and considerate, happy to provide whatever she asked for, and he was pleasant company. And once the house was quiet and they retired for the night, she did her best to convince herself that he loved her, too.

The aroma of chicken roasting met George's nose before he reached the house. His stomach grumbled, and even though he'd eaten a hearty lunch, he was hungry. He was earlier than usual coming back to the house, and he hoped there was a piece of leftover peach pie or a few cookies to hold him over until supper.

He wanted to see Laura, too. He missed her when they were apart, and he'd recently admitted to himself that the best part of his day was when he was alone with her, talking to her, holding her in his arms, kissing her. He'd never thought he'd feel eager to be home again after losing Verna, but every day now, he hurried through his chores as quickly as he could so he could spend the rest of his day with Laura and Alice. And he looked forward to the nights, too, once Alice was asleep and he and Laura were alone.

He had no idea how it had happened, but somehow, Laura had gently eased her way into his heart and now he couldn't imagine his life without her. He wondered if she knew how much she meant to him. He didn't think so, and he was afraid to tell her in case she didn't feel the same way. If she didn't, he didn't want to know. He wanted nothing more than to take care of her, protect her, and spend the rest of his days with her.

He suspected she might, though. He knew Verna had loved him, but she had never responded to his kisses and lovemaking the way Laura did. Surely that meant something, didn't it?

Alice had accepted Laura as her new mother, and he'd already seen changes in how his daughter was behaving. When May was teaching Laura something, Alice was eager to take part, which meant she was learning, too.

Yes, he thought. Life was good. No, not just good. Life was perfect.

And that scared him, because everybody knew that no life could stay perfect forever.

Laughter from the kitchen met his ears when he opened the door and went into the house. He smiled, hung his hat on the hook near the door and followed the sound.

His eyes widened and his smile faded when he went into the kitchen. Two sets of muddy footprints led from the back door to the chair were Alice was sitting. Laura was kneeling at her feet, Alice's foot in her hand while she untied the shoelace. She looked up and smiled at George.

Laura had smudges of dirt on her face, dirt embedded in her fingernails. The hem of the pink dress she was wearing was wet and stained. Her hair, normally pinned into a knot at the nape of her neck, had come loose, curls framing her face. "Supper is ready," she said. "I'll put it on the table as soon as we clean up a little."

He ignored Laura. "What's going on?" His gaze strayed to Alice, who had a jar filled with water and minnows beside her on the table. She was filthy, and grinning.

"Look, Papa," she said, her eyes filled with excitement. "We got minnows so we can go fishing."

Disappointment, and even twinges of anger, filled him. He wouldn't say anything right now, but once they were alone, he was going to demand an explanation why Laura was allowing Alice to behave the way she always had.

Sure, Alice was learning to do the things that were expected of a girl—and eventually a woman—but he'd expected Laura to stop her doing things like…*this!*

"Fishing," he repeated, forcing a smile to is face.

Alice nodded, her blonde curls bouncing and her bright blue eyes wide with excitement. "If it doesn't rain tomorrow."

Laura pulled Alice's mud-covered shoes off and set them on the floor beside the door, then removed her wet socks as well. Then she repeated the process with her own shoes and stockings. "I'll get us both changed," she said to George. "We'll only be a minute."

Taking Alice by the hand, they both left George standing in the kitchen, fuming. Laura was well aware of how he felt about Alice crawling around in mud like a boy, and yet she'd not only allowed it, by her own appearance she'd encouraged it.

He followed them through the house to where they'd disappeared up the stairs and called out, "I'm not hungry. I'm going out and I don't know when I'll be back."

Then he grabbed his hat and left the house, slamming the door behind him.

Laura closed the book she'd been reading to Alice. She'd only had to read two pages before Alice's eyes closed, exhausted from their afternoon by the creek. Laura gently kissed her forehead and turned down the lamp.

It had been a good day. While May was out somewhere with Dutch, Alice had prepared a small picnic lunch for her and Alice and taken her to a clearing beside the creek not far from the house.

The sun had been warm, the birds chirping

happily in the trees, the bees buzzing in the wildflowers. After they'd eaten, they'd taken a stroll along the water's edge. They hadn't gone far when Alice noticed minnows swimming in the shallow water. Alice had asked Laura if they could go fishing, and Laura had almost said no, but a memory from her childhood surfaced and instead, she smiled and nodded. They'd spent the rest of the afternoon collecting the minnows for their fishing expedition the next day.

George was in the parlor reading when she passed him on her way to the kitchen, planning to get a glass of water before she confronted him about the way he'd acted earlier. He hadn't spoken to her since he walked out before supper.

"Laura!" he called out as she crossed the room, stopping to sweep up a few crumbs off the tablecloth with her hand.

She spun around to face him. He was angry. That much was clear by the snipped tone of his voice. "Yes?"

"Don't you think you should apologize for what you did today?"

What? She had nothing to apologize for. If anyone had apologizing to do, it was him. Her brows lifted. "Excuse me? What exactly should I be apologizing for?"

He closed the book and set it down on the table beside him. "I thought we had an agreement that you'd teach Alice to be a lady."

"That's what I have been doing," she countered.

"Do you really think taking her to catch minnows and going fishing is ladylike?"

"Do you really think cooking and doing laundry and cleaning house is the only things a lady should do? Nothing else? She shouldn't have any other interests?"

"Of course not, but—"

"I am teaching her what she'll need to know when she grows up and have a home of her own, but really, George, she's only six years old. There's plenty of time. She needs to be a child, too, and children like to play games and—"

"Then why can't she do things other little girls do, like play with dolls, and…" His voice tapered off.

"What?" Laura asked, her anger fading. "What else should she do?"

He scrubbed his hand through his hair. "I don't know what else little girls do. Don't you know?"

Laura gazed at him, this man who had no idea how to raise a girl. He was angry because he didn't realize girls could like anything other than playing with dolls. Her anger faded a little.

"George, you only heard about the minnows and fishing. You didn't hear about the rest of our afternoon."

"What about it?"

"She helped me prepare the lunch we took on our picnic. She drew a picture, which she wanted to show you but you stormed out before she had a chance. I was knitting, and she asked me to teach her so we'll start lessons tomorrow. All of that was before she saw the minnows in the creek."

"Oh…"

Laura came to sit beside him and shifted to face him. "When I was little, about Alice's age or maybe a little older, I was in my bedroom trying to learn how to make the perfect lazy daisy stitch on a pillowcase. I looked out the window and saw my three cousins heading toward the river with fishing poles and a bucket of bait.

"I so wanted to go with them, but I knew I'd never be allowed to, because my parents thought the way you do. So I sneaked out and followed them, and hid in the bushes beside the river. I envied them so much. It wasn't that I didn't like embroidery, but I wanted to do more than that and they were having so much fun, I wanted to do that, too."

The tension she'd seen in George's jaw seemed to relax. Just a little, but she wondered if maybe he was starting to understand.

"I got stung by a wasp, and when I let out a shriek, the boys knew I was there. They showed me what to do, and it was one of the best afternoons of my life—until my governess found me. She locked me in my room until I promised to 'learn to be a lady'."

Sympathy appeared in George's eyes. "That's terrible."

"George," Laura said softly, "of course I'll teach Alice proper etiquette, and how to act and speak, but there's really nothing wrong with going fishing, or climbing a tree once in a while. A person doesn't have to be all male or all female. There are shades of each in everybody, if they let themselves admit it."

"No, there isn't—"

Laura smiled. "Really? What about John Weaver? He obviously loves to cook if he owns a diner. Isn't that women's work?"

"Well…" George sputtered. "That's different."

"Is it? What about Maude Ramsay? Doesn't she cut hair and give shaves alongside her husband? Does that make her less of a woman?"

"Well…no…"

"Give Alice time," Laura said. "She'll be fine."

He sighed. "I'm just worried that she'll grow up with no friends, and she won't be able to find a husband."

"She has a new friend. And you'll be pleased to know it's a girl."

"She does?"

Laura nodded. "I ran into Miss Coleridge the other day when I was in town and she told me about a new family in town who have a daughter Alice's age. They eat lunch together and now even some of the other girls join them. So you see, you have nothing to worry about."

"Then I guess it's me who should be apologizing for walking out."

"Yes, it is."

"Then I'm sorry. I'll have to learn to trust your judgment."

Laura chuckled. "Good. Now come into the kitchen and let me fix you a plate. You must be hungry."

"I am." He stood, reached down and took Laura's hand, keeping it buried in his until they reached the kitchen.

Laura shivered as she made her way to the chicken coop. Winter was coming, but George assured her it never got cold enough for snow, and he'd asked her what snow felt like because he'd never seen it. She'd tried to describe it, but it was impossible, so he'd promised that one Christmas, they'd take a trip to Michigan so that they could spend the holidays with her family and he could see snow for himself.

Laura was happy, mostly. She loved George and Alice with all her heart. She'd made friends with many of the ladies in town, and she loved living in Sapphire Springs. There was only one thing she still wanted, still needed.

She wanted George to love her. He showed her every day how much he appreciated everything she did for them, and she *thought* he cared about her, but she was finding it wasn't enough.

May and Dutch had decided to get married in the spring, and seeing them together, so much in love, only emphasized what was missing in Laura's marriage.

She was glad that George was spending more time than usual away from the house these days. She'd been knitting gifts for everyone so whenever she got the chance, she'd knit a few rows.

She'd also been teaching Alice to knit. Alice had decided she wanted to make her father a scarf for Christmas. She chose the yarn, and Laura helped her to cast on. The tension in Alice's stitches wasn't perfect, and she often dropped a stitch that Laura had to fix, but she kept going.

"My scarf isn't pretty like yours," Alice complained one afternoon, throwing the half-finished scarf on the floor.

Laura picked it up and put it beside Alice on the settee. "It's even better than mine," she said.

Alice's lips pouted and her eyes narrowed. "No it isn't. Mine has holes. See?" She dug a finger through the space between two stitches that were looser than the others.

"It's because of those holes that it is special. And your papa is going to love it even if it's full of holes."

"He will?"

Laura nodded. "Because you made it especially for him. Anybody can go to a store to buy a gift or order something from a catalog, but you gave up the time you could have spent playing with your toys or doing something else for yourself to make something that nobody else will ever have, that makes it very special."

"But you made a scarf, too."

"Yes, I did." Laura picked up the scarf Alice was working on. "But I didn't make *this* scarf. And when it's finished, there will be never be another scarf exactly like this one. And your papa will be the only man in the world to have a scarf like this."

Alice cocked her head to the side as she thought about what Laura had said. "He will," she finally said.

"But you have to finish it," Laura pointed out.

"Okay, but I can I have a cookie first."

Laura set down her knitting beside Alice's and smiled. "I think a milk and cookie break is just what we both need."

Laura was surprised when she looked out the kitchen window and saw George riding toward the barn early one afternoon the week before Christmas. He'd told her that morning that he'd be spending the day out in the north pasture fixing the fence that had blown down in the storm a few nights before. She'd prepared a cold lunch for him and sent him on his way.

Alice was at school, and May had gone to town to buy supplies for the Christmas baking they planned to do the next day.

She stood at the window, peeling the potatoes for

supper and watching as he disappeared into the barn. She finished preparing the potatoes and covered them with cold water.

What was he doing out there, she wondered, her curiosity piqued? She missed him when he was gone, so she put the pot on the stove to cook later and headed outside to the barn.

She stepped inside, giving herself a few seconds to let her eyes adjust to the dim light in the barn after coming in from the bright sunshine.

She couldn't see him anywhere. "George?"

There was no answer.

She called his name again, worry taking hold and snaking through her veins. Where was he?

Walking slowly and stopping to check every horse stall and look behind every piece of equipment stored there, she was almost at the back of the barn when she saw him. Or rather, she saw one of his legs on the floor, sticking out from the gate of one of the stalls.

Her heart somersaulted in her chest, almost choking her with fear as she hurried toward him.

He was sprawled face down on the straw, his head to the side, his eyes closed.

She crouched down beside him. "George! George! Wake up!"

His eyes fluttered open. He braced himself on his hands and tried to get up, but he was too weak and dropped back onto the straw. "What happened?"

"You fainted," Laura said, reaching down to help him get to his feet.

"I wasn't feeling good so I came back. That's the last I remember."

Laura laid her hand on his forehead for a moment. He was burning up! "We need to get you into the house. You have a fever."

It took ten minutes for him to make it into the house. Laura managed to get his boots off but she left him in his clothes and got him into bed. He curled up into a ball, shivering.

She'd never seen anyone in this condition before, and it shook her to her core. She had to do something, but she wasn't sure what. The only thing she was sure of was that he needed a doctor. "George, are any of the men working around the house today?"

He didn't answer for a few seconds and she wondered if he'd fallen asleep—or worse—but then he muttered, "Think…Bobby…fixing a wheel…" His eyes closed.

She was afraid to leave him, but she had no choice. Hurrying outside, she ran to the shed where she hoped to find Bobby. Luckily, he was there, and within minutes, he was riding toward town, leaving Laura praying George wouldn't die before the doctor arrived.

For the next three days, Laura barely left George's side. May brought meals to the bedside and took care of Alice and the other chores around the house.

The nights were the worst, when the house was quiet. She sat in the chair beside the bed, dozing, keeping a cold cloth on his forehead and giving him sips of water when he was conscious enough to swallow. The rest of the time, she watched him breathe while he thrashed and mumbled in his delirium.

The doctor had no idea what was wrong with him, so couldn't even assure her he'd survive.

Early one evening, May came into the room. "Laura, Alice is really upset. She needs to see her father. I know you're afraid that whatever illness George has might be contagious, but she thinks he's dead like her mother and there's nothing I can say to convince her he's still alive."

Laura gazed down at George, lying so still in the bed. He was so pale, his jaw shadowed with dark hair. Her heart ached. She loved him, loved him more than she'd ever thought it was possible to love a man. If he died… Her throat tightened and tears stung her eyes.

Laura took George's hand in both of hers, willing him to fight for his life. "I love you," she whispered. "I love you so much. And Alice loves you. We need you to come back to us."

He couldn't die. He just couldn't.

Raised voices from the other room filtered into her thoughts.

"I hate her!" That was Alice's voice. What was she so upset about? Laura listened, realizing it was her Alice was talking about.

May's voice, quieter than Alice's but still loud

enough that Laura could hear, filtered through the closed door. "Hush, Alice." She said. "You don't want to wake your Papa. He's very sick and needs to rest."

Laura listened as the voices grew louder.

"He went to Heaven, didn't he?"

"No."

Alice was sobbing, almost hysterically. "I want my papa!"

"Your mama will let you see him when he's better. Now stop shouting."

"No! I hate her! I want my papa!"

A soft knock sounded at the door a moment before it opened and May stepped inside. "I'm sorry, Laura. I'm trying to keep Alice calm, but—"

"It's all right, May. I heard her."

"She wants to see George. She's still convinced he's dead. She told me that he wouldn't let her see her mother when she got sick and that's because she died. Maybe you should let her at least see him so that she can see he's still alive."

"I think you're right," Laura replied, "but I want to talk to her first. I don't want her to be even more upset when she comes in here and sees him like this."

May nodded. "I'll sit with George until you come back."

"Thanks," Laura said, and then got up and left the room.

CHAPTER 15

"You must be very quiet so you don't wake him," Laura said to Alice a few minutes later when she took her into the bedroom where George was sleeping. "He needs to rest."

"But I need to talk to him," Alice protested.

"Later," Laura told her. "Not right now."

Alice took a few steps closer to the bed, taking in deep shuddery breaths. Then she looked up at Laura, tears spiking her lashes and staining her cheeks. "He's not dead?"

"No," Laura said. "He's just sleeping." Laura took Alice's hand and laid it on his chest. "See? He's breathing."

Alice stood beside the bed, staring down at her father for long moments. Then she looked up at Laura. "Is Papa going to go to Heaven like my mama?"

Laura's heart twisted. If only she knew. She was doing everything she could to make sure he didn't die, but even the doctor wasn't sure he'd survive whatever this illness was.

She couldn't lie to Alice, but she couldn't tell her he still might die. "I don't know."

As soon as the words left her mouth, she realized that hadn't eased Alice's fears at all. Her eyes widened and the tears filled her eyes again and ran down her cheeks. "But you have to make him not go to Heaven."

How could she explain that she had no control, that whether he lived or died was out of her hands? "I can't—"

Alice's voice grew louder and her face flushed. "My mama died and now she lives in Heaven and now I can't see her anymore. I don't want my papa to go to Heaven."

Laura's eyes stung with unshed tears. She couldn't break down now. She had to be strong for Alice. She didn't want George to die either. If he did… How would she survive without him?

"You have to make him not die," Alice repeated. "Promise."

Laura shook her head. "I can't promise that."

Alice's eyes narrowed and her lips pressed together. Her fear and sorrow had given way to anger. "You want him to die!"

"No! No—I don't…"

Alice looked up at her, tears streaming down her cheeks and loathing in her eyes. "I hate you," she screamed at the top of her lungs. Then she spun around and stormed out of the room.

George was cold. So cold. And so tired. Was this what dying felt like? Memories floated in and out of his brain—his father teaching him how to saddle a horse, his mother reading to him at bedtime, time, Verna…

Verna. Their wedding day, the day Alice was born, the day she left him. He'd begged her to fight to stay with him, but she'd gazed up at him, and in a weak voice, said, "I love you," and then closed her eyes for the last time.

Now he could see her, smiling at him, moving toward him. She looked healthy, happy.

Through his fevered haze, he heard himself call out her name as he tried to touch her, to hold her, but she was always just out of reach.

Then Laura's face floated into his mind. Laura, the women he'd fallen in love with. He hadn't wanted to, hadn't planned to, but it had happened. And now he might die without her knowing how he felt.

He felt a cool hand on his and sensed deep down that it was Laura's hand.

"Please don't die, George," she whispered. "I can't go on without you."

He wanted so badly to open his eyes, to tell her he loved her, that he wanted to live, but he was just too tired.

~

Laura stayed at George's bedside that night. His fever was worse, and he began to thrash around. She sponged him down with cold water, carefully spooned the medicine the doctor had left into his mouth, and waited

Every few minutes, he threw off the blankets as his skin burned, but then he began shivering so badly she had to cover him again.

She was terrified! He was dying. She was sure of it. And there was nothing she could do to prevent it.

In his delirium, he started to speak, so softly she could barely hear him. She talked softly, urging him to rest, but no matter what she did, she couldn't calm him.

"…Ver…" she heard him say, the word barely more than a breath.

He was calling to his wife. Her heart squeezed, the pain in her heart almost unbearable.

"…ever…love…"

"Verna…" The word was only a whisper as the fever swept through him. "Forever…love…"

The lump forming in Laura's throat almost choked her as the realization hit her that he still loved his wife, that he would never love her. She'd thought he was starting to love her as much as she loved him, but she'd been wrong. So wrong.

She couldn't do it! She couldn't live with George a minute longer, sure now that he'd never love her. She'd thought she could be satisfied with his friendship, but it wasn't enough. It would be unbearable to spend the rest of her life with him, knowing his heart would always belong to another woman.

Tears spilled from her eyes, and she let them fall.

The first rays of dawn were lighting the day when George's fever broke and he fell into a more restful sleep.

Laura got up, gently touched his lips with hers, and wiped away one of her tears that had fallen onto his cheek. "Goodbye, George."

Then she went into the kitchen to tell May what she was planning to do. May looked up from the bread she was slicing on the table. Her eyes widened when she saw Laura's tears. "Did George—?"

"No," Laura replied.

"Then what's wrong?" May asked,

"The doctor told me that George's fever would spike and he'd either die or recover," Laura said. "His fever has dropped, so it looks like he'll be fine."

May put down the knife and hugged Laura.

"That's wonderful news, so why are you crying? Happy tears?"

Laura shook her head. "I know I'm asking a lot, but can you do something for me?"

"Of course," May replied. "Anything."

Laura could barely get the words out past the tightness in her throat and chest. "Take care of Alice and George until he's well?"

May's forehead puckered. "Why? Where are you going?"

"I'm leaving."

"What?"

"I can't stay here," Laura said, then explained what she'd heard during the night.

"But—"

"Please do this for me," Laura begged. "It's too painful to love someone the way I love George and know that he's in love with someone else, especially when that someone is dead. I just can't do it a day longer."

"Where will you go?" May asked.

Laura shook her head. "I don't know. I just know I need to leave. Now."

Sympathy shone out of May's eyes, and Laura was grateful to have a friend like her.

May nodded. "You know I'll help you any way I can, and once Dutch and I are married, you're welcome to come and stay with us as long as you want to."

Laura let out a weak laugh. "Don't you think you should ask Dutch about that before you offer?"

"No," May replied. "Because if he would turn his back on my best friend, I don't want him."

Laura reached out and hugged May again. "Thank you," she murmured.

CHAPTER 16

George's eyes fluttered open. The room was bathed in golden light, and he gingerly moved his head to look out the window where the sun was hugging the horizon. Sunrise or sunset? He didn't know.

He was tired and as weak as a newborn calf, but he was alive. The last thing he remembered was Laura helping him into the house. How long ago was that?

The house was quiet. Where was everyone? He tried to call out for Laura but his throat was so dry all that came out was a croak.

It must have been loud enough because a few seconds later, the door opened and May walked in. When she saw George, she gave him a wide smile. "You're awake!"

He nodded, that small movement exhausting him.

He closed his eyes for a moment. "Laura?" he asked. "Where's Laura?"

Even though he hadn't been able to talk to Laura while he was so sick, he'd felt her presence, and a few times, he thought he'd even heard her telling him she loved him.

He didn't know if she'd really said that or if it was nothing more than a feverish dream, but he needed to know, and the only way to do that was to ask her.

The expression on May's face was unreadable. What was going on?

"You must be thirsty," May said. "Let me get you some water and then we'll talk." She disappeared and came back a minute later with a glass of water. She perched on the side of the bed and help him raise his head enough to take a sip.

The coolness against his parched throat felt wonderful and he wanted more, but she took the glass away. "May—"

"A few sips at a time, George," she said, "or else you'll get sick."

He nodded weakly and relaxed against the pillow. "Now tell me, where's Laura and Alice?"

"Alice is still sleeping," May replied. "She'll be so happy to see you're awake. She was really worried."

"I'm not surprised," George agreed. "She probably thought I was going to die, too." He let out a weak laugh. "I did, too. And Laura? Is she still sleeping, too?

May looked away and didn't answer immediately.

What was going on? Finally, she met his gaze. "She's gone."

George's heart somersaulted in his chest and a cold chill washed over him.

A lump formed in his throat, his nose stung and he blinked back the salty tears that threatened to flow.

He remembered Verna appearing in his dreams, smiling softly, telling him it wasn't his time to stay with her, and that he needed to go back, to move on and let himself love again. It was then he'd realized he'd fallen in love with Laura, and even though Verna would always hold a place in his heart as his first love and mother of his child, Laura was his future.

And now it was too late

His voice cracked when he spoke again. "Did…is she already buried?"

May's eyes widened. "What?

"The funeral," he said.

"What funeral?"

Was he hallucinating? Why didn't May understand what he was asking.

"Laura's funeral," he said, his voice growing impatient.

May looked at him as if he'd gone mad. "Why would there be a funeral for Laura? She's not dead."

He was confused. Had the fever done something to his brain? Hadn't May just said she'd died? "You said she was gone."

"Oh…" May smiled then. "I'm sorry. Bad choice of words. She's very much alive."

The grief, the pain that had overwhelmed him suddenly cleared. "Thank God," he murmured. "I thought she'd gotten sick too and died. But then, if she's alive, where is she?"

"I hate to be the one to tell you, but she left."

"What do you mean, she left?"

"She's living in town so that she can still spend time with Alice, but—"

"She doesn't want to be with me."

"I'm sorry, George."

Just then, he heard an excited squeal and Alice raced into the room. May grabbed her moments before she pounced on George's chest. "Easy, Alice," May said kindly. "Your papa has been very sick and we need to be gentle with him, okay?"

"Okay," Alice agreed.

George opened is arms and May released her. Carefully, Alice climbed onto the bed and snuggled against his chest. Her small fingers rubbed the scruffy beard that was growing on his jaw. "You still sick, Papa?"

"I'm getting better," he replied, "and seeing you makes me feel much better. Right now, though, I'm really tired."

May picked Alice off the bed. "Let's go have breakfast and let your papa have a nap and then you can visit again."

Alice nodded. "Okay."

George forced himself to smile as they left the room. As the door closed behind them, his smile faded. His chest tightened and his throat thickened to the point he could barely swallow past the lump in his throat.

Laura had left him.

Rain spattered against the window of Laura's room at Mrs. Lake's boarding house in Sapphire Springs. She'd been there for almost a week, barely leaving the room. This morning, she lay in the bed, staring absently at the window as the raindrops made tracks down the window.

Today would be the first time since she left the ranch that she wouldn't see Alice, and the day stretched endlessly in front of her.

Spending time with Alice was the only bright spot in her days now that she'd left the ranch. Every day at noon, Laura walked over to the schoolhouse at the other end of town and waited for the bell to ring. Then she sat with Alice and her friends until it was time for them to go back inside, listening to their chattering and eager for any tidbit of news about George that Alice might say.

After replaying everything that had happened, Laura had finally admitted to herself that she'd been wrong to leave George the way she had. She'd been so hurt by his admission that he would always love Verna that she'd reacted irrationally.

She should have waited until he was well, when

she could explain to him why she was leaving. Instead, she'd run away because she didn't have the courage to face him and tell him the truth.

She'd been a coward. Such a coward. For that, she would never forgive herself.

The guilt had weighed on her so much that it had affected her health. She didn't feel well, hadn't felt well for a few days now. She wondered if she had a mild case of the same illness that made George so ill, but even if it was, she really had to stop feeling sorry for herself and start looking for employment some-where. She still had money she'd brought with her from back East, but that wouldn't last forever.

Would her shattered heart ever mend, she wondered. Would there ever come a time when she wouldn't miss George so much she wanted to just curl up and die?

A knock sounded at her door. Her nerves skittered through her. Maybe it was George…

Laura bounded out of bed, and a moment later regretted her sudden movement. Nausea bubbled up inside her. With a moan, she dropped to her knees and reached under the bed, grabbing the empty chamber pot with no time to spare.

"Mrs. Cowan," Mrs. Lake's voice filtered through the door as she knocked again. "Are you all right?"

She couldn't answer, and a few seconds later, the door opened and Mrs. Lake came inside.

Laura was sitting on the floor, sucking in short breaths, her back leaning against the bed.

"Oh my goodness," Mrs. Lake exclaimed, rushing to her side. "You poor thing. Here, let me help you up and get you into bed."

Laura took the hand Mrs. Lake offered and struggled to her feet, then collapsed on the side of the bed. "I don't know what came over me..."

Mrs. Lake rested her palm on Laura's forehead. "You don't have a fever and it's not likely it's something you ate because you've barely eaten enough to keep a bird alive since you've been here."

"I haven't been very hungry," Laura muttered.

"I don't pry into my guests' business, but you seem so unhappy," Mrs. Lake said, patting Laura's hand. "If you want to talk about it, I'm here."

The tears Laura couldn't seem to control threatened again, but she managed to blink them back. "Thank you."

"Do you feel better now?" Mrs. Lake asked.

Laura nodded. "I don't know what's wrong with me."

"I think I do," Mrs. Lake said, smiling. "I think you might be expecting."

Laura's brows lifted. "What? No...I mean..."

"I'm going to bring you some breakfast," Mrs. Lake said.

"I'm not hungry—"

"Think about it while I'm gone. If you are with child, you need to eat, to keep your strength up, and for your baby."

A few seconds later, the door closed behind her landlady.

Laura got up and crossed to the window, absently looking through the rain-spattered glass to the street below. Was it possible? Could she really be expecting a child? George's child?

She had to admit, until George got sick, they'd made love almost every night. It made sense that eventually… And when she really thought about it, it had been some time since her last menses. The realization hit her. She was going to have a baby!

"Oh, no…" she whispered to the empty room. She looked down and splayed her hand across her abdomen. She'd hoped that one day, she'd give George a child, but not now, not the way things were.

What was she going to do? She'd seen how much George loved Alice, and she was sure he'd love a child of theirs, too. She couldn't deprive him of his child. And she couldn't deprive her child of a father.

She knew what she had to do. She'd go and see the doctor, and if what she now suspected was true, she'd have no choice. For her child's sake and George's, she'd go back to the ranch and spend the rest of her life pretending—even to herself—that her life was perfect.

George sucked in a deep breath as he rolled over and managed to get his legs over the side of the bed. Using what little strength he had in his arms, he forced himself to a sitting position. That small movement exhausted him, and he had to sit for a few minutes to catch his breath.

He was still so weak. Whatever had ailed him wasn't going away as quickly as he needed it to. Slowly, carefully, he rose to his feet and by hanging onto the bed posts and the bureau for support, he managed to make it to the chair at the window.

"May?" he called out. He hated having to rely on May, especially for his personal needs, but he had no choice.

A few seconds later, May came into the room, wiping her hands on a cloth. "How are you feeling this morning?"

"Better every day," he said. "Can you bring me

some paper and a pencil, too?" he asked. "I want to write a note to Laura. I want her to come back to me."

May didn't move. "That won't work, George."

"Why not?"

"I have a confession to make," she said, a flush creeping into her cheeks.

A frown creased his forehead. "What did you do?"

"I asked Dutch to sit with you a couple of days ago while you were asleep and I went into town to see Laura. I told her how miserable you were about her leaving and that you wanted her to come back home. She refused."

She turned to leave the room.

"Then what can I do?" he asked her retreating figure.

She came back into the room. "Why do you want her to come back?"

"Because…"

"Because what, George?" May prodded.

"Because I love her," he murmured.

"Sorry, I didn't hear you."

He faced May's gaze head-on. "I love her, okay?"

"Then why didn't you tell her that when she was here?" May asked.

He shook his head. "I…I didn't want to love her. I was scared—"

"Papa!" Alice appeared in the doorway and ran to him, throwing her arms around his waist and snuggling into his chest.

He wrapped Alice in his arms and kissed the top of her head. A moment later, she pulled away. "What are you scared of, Papa?"

"Nothing."

"Remember when I fell off Sunny when I was little and I hurt my backside and I was scared to ride her again and you said that when you're scared of something, you just have to do it over and over until you're not scared anymore and I did and now I'm not scared to ride Sunny anymore."

He gazed down at his daughter. He'd forgotten about the tiny spill she'd taken a few months before. Now she was throwing his words back at him. And she was right.

If he'd really heard Laura telling him she loved him that night while he was delirious with fever, then she'd still love him now. Wouldn't she?

He had to find out. May had told him she was living at Mrs. Lake's boarding house in town.

"Miss May says you still see your mama." It was more of a question than a statement.

Alice nodded. "She comes to my school when the bell rings."

"She does?"

Alice nodded. "I wish she still lived here, but she said she can't."

"Me too." Turning back to May, he said, "Can you ask Dutch to hitch the wagon? I'm going into town."

"You're not ready——"

"I'm not waiting one more day."

May grinned. "I'll go an ask him right now."

George leaned over to meet Alice at her eye level. "Do you want to go into town with me?"

Alice nodded, her ringlets bouncing.

George straightened and took Alice's hand in his. "Then let's go and bring your mama home."

Laura was folding one of her dresses when a knock came to the door. She opened it to find Mrs. Lake there. "You have visitors downstairs," she said.

"Thank you," Laura said. "I'll be right there." She closed the door and quickly ran a comb through her hair before pinning it into place.

She couldn't imagine who would be calling on her. During her time in Sapphire Springs, she'd made many friends, but how many of them had heard that she was now living in town? She trusted Mrs. Lake's discretion, so she doubted the woman had told anyone. The only other person who knew was May, and Mrs. Lake would have allowed May to come upstairs.

She glanced down at her dress, smoothing out a crease before leaving the room and hurrying down the stairs.

Her heart skipped a beat when she walked into the parlor and saw George sitting on the settee. He was pale, his eyes tired. He'd lost weight, making his features more pronounced. But he was still the most handsome man she'd ever known.

He stood up as she approached, but slumped back onto the seat, a sure sign he was still weak from his illness. Alice was sitting beside him, her hands clasped daintily in her lap.

It took all her self-control to appear calm and impersonal. "Good morning," she said, forcing a lightness into her voice she didn't feel.

Alice jumped up and ran to Laura. "Mama," Alice said, excitement in her voice, "Papa says you're going to come home with us."

George's eyes widened. "Alice!"

He looked at Laura, shaking his head. "I'm so sorry. I didn't—"

"It's fine," Laura interrupted, meeting his gaze, noticing the reddish tint of embarrassment coloring his cheeks. She crouched to Alice's eye level. "Excuse me for a moment," she said, then spun around and left the room.

She found Mrs. Lake in the kitchen. "I hate to impose, but would you mind—"

The landlady grinned "Not at all," she replied, then left Laura standing in the kitchen while she went into the parlor. Laura heard her speak to Alice. "How would you like a cookie and a glass of milk?"

As Laura entered the parlor, she saw Alice looking at her father, who nodded. Seconds later, Mrs. Lake and Alice were gone and Laura was alone with George.

She almost laughed. She was almost as nervous now as she'd been that first day when she arrived on the train. "How are you feeling?" she asked. She was determined to keep their conversation casual, even though her heart was breaking with every breath. She didn't know how she was supposed to spend the rest of her life feeling like this every minute of every day, but somehow, she had to.

"I'm getting better," he replied.

She gave him a faint smile. "I'm glad."

Silence fell over the room. Finally, she was about to ask the question hanging in the air when George spoke. "Laura, I…I want you to come home."

She didn't answer immediately. She was planning to go back, but for some reason she couldn't explain, she was hesitant to say so. There would be time to tell him everything later.

"Please," he added. When he saw she wasn't going to answer, he closed the gap between them and took her hands. His thumbs grazed her palms, and heat streaked through her.

Even now, when she knew she'd never be the woman he loved, she couldn't resist him. She met his dark gaze, and she thought she saw something different in his eyes, something she didn't recognize.

"I can't…I mean…I need you. I miss you. And…" His voice cracked, but he smiled anyway. "And I love you."

For one of the few times in her life, Laura was

speechless. She couldn't have heard him right. "What?"

He nodded. "I love you so much," he repeated. "Please come back to me."

"But how…when…?"

"I tried so hard not to love you, because when Verna died…" he began.

Laura pulled her hands away, that sharp pang of rejection stabbing her again. For a few seconds, she'd believed him and she'd been overwhelmed with joy, only to be slammed back into reality. "No, you don't love me," she said, stepping back. "When you were delirious with fever, I heard you calling out to her, telling her you'd love her forever."

"I said that?"

"Well…"

His expression darkened. "Tell me exactly what I said."

She repeated the words she'd heard. "Are you going to deny it?"

George's brows drew together. "I won't deny I said those words, but I said more than that. I remember it clearly. I thought I'd died when I saw her. She was moving toward me, telling me I needed to go back. I told her I wanted to, because I'd fallen in love with you. I did tell her she will always have a small piece of my heart, because that's true. She was my first love, she was the mother of my child, but the rest of my heart belongs to you. Now and forever. Those were the words you heard."

Laura wanted to believe him, but she was afraid to. But if he was telling the truth…

George took her hands again, his grip tighter so she couldn't escape. "Laura, listen to me," he said. "When Verna died, I was devastated. I thought my life was over. But you brought me back to life. I was afraid to love again, but even though I fought it all the way, somehow, you wrapped yourself around my heart and wouldn't let go. Do you believe me?"

She nodded.

"While I was sick, I thought I heard you say you loved me," he went on. "Was I hallucinating?"

Laura looked up at him through a blur of tears. This time, they were happy tears. "No, you weren't. I do love you, too."

He drew her into his arms and kissed her, a kiss unlike any other they'd shared. A kiss filled with love.

When he released her, she gazed up at him through a blur of tears, but this time they were happy tears.

"I want to spend my life with you, have children with you and—"

Laura grinned. "About that," she said, her heart so filled with joy she was afraid it might explode.

His brows lifted and his expression grew serious. "What about it?"

"I saw the doctor, and it seems one of those children you want should arrive in about seven months."

George's mouth gaped open for a second before his arms went around her and he kissed her again, this time with such tenderness that her tears flowed down her cheeks.

One day she might tell him that she'd planned to come back to him anyway, but not right now.

A sound penetrated the fog she was in and it was only when George released her that she saw Alice standing off to the side of the room. She was clapping her hands loudly.

"Papa?"

George held out his arm for Alice. She snuggled beside them and he wrapped his arms around them both. "Ready?" he whispered into Laura's ear.

She nodded and smiled. "Yes," she said. "I'm more than ready. Let's go home."

"**A**re you sure you'll be all right to stand beside me today?" May asked.

Laura gazed down at her slightly swollen stomach. She laughed. May had been a mother hen since she'd heard the news about Laura's pregnancy.

"I'm fine," Laura assured her. "The baby isn't due for another three months. Now let's get you to the church and get you married."

George and Dutch were in the kitchen when Laura went downstairs to tell them May was ready. The men were going to leave first, and May, Laura and Alice would follow. "May is almost ready so you should probably leave now."

"Yeah…yeah…okay…" Dutch was pacing, and Laura couldn't contain her smile. "You look very handsome, Dutch."

"I hope I don't muck up the vows," he said. "I've been trying to memorize them."

"You'll do just fine, I'm sure. And even if you do muck them up, it doesn't matter. May will love you anyway," she said with a chuckle.

Dutch nodded and turned to George. "Again, I can't…I mean, thank you again for everything you've done for May and me. I never thought I'd ever own my own land."

George had deeded a hundred acres to Dutch as a wedding gift. Their house still needed a few finishing touches, but was livable.

"You're my best friend and May is Laura's so we had to make sure you were always close by," George said.

"We're not going anywhere," Dutch told him.

"Except right now we need to get to the church," Laura put in.

A few seconds later, the two men left the room. Laura was at the bottom of the stairs when George came back into the house.

"Did you forget something?" she asked.

He nodded. "I forgot to tell you how beautiful you look today," he said, gently running his hand over her stomach. "And how much I love you and our baby."

"I love you, too," Laura replied. She felt a slight kick from the baby and laughed. "And the baby says he or she loves you, too."

He gazed at her for a long moment. "Do you wish you could have had a real wedding like May and Dutch are going to have?"

Laura shook her head. "I admit that at the time I

did, but not now. We might not have started out the way most people do, but I've realized the wedding itself isn't what's important. It's the love and the life we build together that matters."

He kissed her then, and she knew that no matter what the future brought, with each other, their children and their friends beside them, life would be as perfect as it could possibly be.

Cassie, the sixth book in the Mail-Order Brides of Sapphire Springs, is available now.

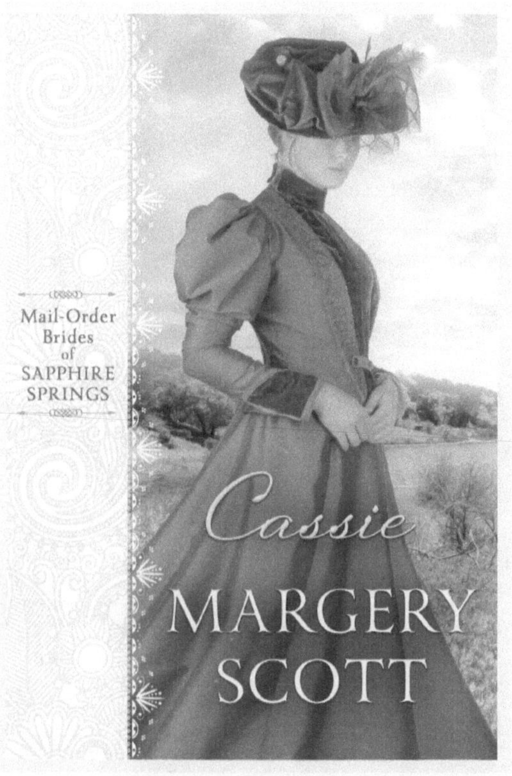

When Cassie travels to Texas as a mail-order bride, she's met with information that changes all her plans. She has no choice but to go back East. Or does she?

ABOUT THE AUTHOR

Margery Scott is the author of more than thirty sweet western historical novels, novellas and short stories. An avid reader, she didn't even consider writing her own books until her three boys were grown and she had an empty nest.

She now lives on a lake in Canada with her husband, and when she's not writing or traveling in search of the perfect setting for her next novel, you can usually find her wielding a pair of knitting needles or a pool cue.

Website: www.margeryscott.com
Email: margery@margeryscott.com
Newsletter: www.margeryscott.com/newsletter
VIP Facebook reader group: www.
facebook.com/groups/margeryscott